SABOTAGE

THE DEPARTMENT Z SERIES

The Death Miser

Redhead

First Came a Murder

Death Round the Corner

The Mark of the Crescent

Thunder in Europe

The Terror Trap

Carriers of Death

Days of Danger

Death Stands By

Menace

Murder Must Wait

Panic!

Death by Night

The Island of Peril

Sabotage

Go Away Death

The Day of Disaster

Prepare for Action

No Darker Crime

Dark Peril

The Peril Ahead

The League of Dark Men

The Department of Death

The Enemy Within

Dead or Alive

A Kind of Prisoner

The Black Spiders

SABOTAGE

DEPARTMENT Z

JOHN CREASEY

OPEN ROAD

INTEGRATED MEDIA

NEW YORK

Copyright © 1941 by John Creasey

ISBN: 978-1-5040-9219-7

This edition published in 2024 by Open Road Integrated Media, Inc.
180 Maiden Lane
New York, NY 10038
www.openroadmedia.com

SABOTAGE

1
LOVELY LADY

M y firm and unalterable opinion is that she's the loveliest pretty I've seen for three months, a week and three days," said Michael Errol. He was clearly at great pains to keep his voice low, although it seemed on occasions that the effect of a moderately thirsty evening would defeat his purpose. Perhaps one word in ten was clear enough for the seven other occupants of Cherry's bar to hear. Moreover he looked frequently past his cousin's shoulder at the woman sitting alone. "Take her eyes, blue as the stars . . ."

"Stars aren't blue," said Mark Errol in a voice which suggested that he was soon to lose his temper with his talkative cousin.

"I am speaking in a poetic sense," said Mike reproachfully. "How can mundane words describe a sleeping beauty. . . ?"

"She isn't sleeping."

"She looks tired," said Mike gently. "She *should* be sleeping. Ever struck you how difficult it must be for a beautiful woman?"

"No," said Mark with acerbity, "but it's struck me how

much better life would be if you would stop burbling." He glanced at his watch, and frowned. "It's nearly half-past seven. We ought to be on our way."

"On our way?" demanded Mike. "Don't be an idiot, we needn't leave for another five minutes."

Mark smiled drily. "Speaking in a poetic sense, of course, what is five minutes?" He rose to his feet, a tall large man, and one good to look upon. Gently he steered his cousin to the door.

The woman whose eyes were sleepy and yet who was nearly as beautiful as Mike had attempted to describe, did not look towards them. She seemed, in fact, to be wrapped in thought.

Leaving the bar at last, Mike and Mark Errol turned into one of the many narrow streets between Piccadilly and Regent Street.

It was late spring and the evening was warm, while the hour of black-out was some time off. People still lolled at ease on the grass of Green Park; many were in uniform, most with the steel helmets and service gas-masks which declared them members of the civilian army.

The Errol cousins did not carry gas-masks.

Moreover they were in lounge suits, and thus they called for some comment from people who watched them—older folk, for the most part, in whom the spirit of 1914–18 was strong, and who could not understand that a lounge suit could be as much a symbol of service as a uniform.

The attitude of the white-haired old gentleman who came towards them as they strolled was the more forgivable since they were so tall and large and clearly in good health. They were remarkably alike and were often mistaken for twins; feature by feature there was little to distinguish them from one another. High forehead, with hair growing rather far back, but crisp and plentiful. Straight noses perhaps a little long, wide and full lips and somewhat massive, even aggressive chins. They were hatless that evening, and thus it was easier to tell Mike from Mark, for Mark's hair, always a little more unruly than his cousin's, was cut a little shorter and was a shade—no more than a shade—darker.

Both walked with long, slow steps; both appeared to have no care or concern in the world. The white-haired gentleman approached them rapidly. Fierce blue eyes glared at them from a reddish countenance. Words came explosively. "Aren't you *ashamed* of yourselves?"

Mike looked at Mark, together they regarded the old one. "Should we be?"

"Certainly you should," snapped the old one, and he was breathing heavily, he was more than indignant, he was ashamed for them. "Every man worth his salt is fighting—*fighting*—there is no room in the Empire for sluggards who do nothing, who find for themselves reserved occupations . . ."

Mark looked at Mike, then: "Aren't you rather jumping to conclusions, sir?"

The old man's fury wavered. Something in the faces of those he accused gave him the lie. He still was not sure, but doubt was there. "Well, if I've been too hasty, you must forgive an old soldier," he said gruffly. He seemed to dwindle.

They bowed together and walked on. Mike grinned, but Mark was frowning, for he took things harder than his cousin.

"Damned old fool," he said.

"Oh, I don't know. Good intentions and all that," said Mike.

"Good intentions! Interfering old busybody. I've a good mind to ask him what he's doing . . ."

It was Mike's turn to lay a hand on his cousin's arm.

"Not just now you don't," he said. "Forget it, man, anyone would think your conscience was uneasy and he'd caught it on a sore spot." Very suddenly Mike began to laugh, and after a pause his cousin's face cleared and they laughed together. It put them in a good humour, for the situation had its funny side. They wondered—although they were not twins they had similar thoughts at similar times on many things—what the old one would have felt had he known the truth.

Almost certainly he would not have believed it, and would have declared that Department Z, to which they belonged, was a melodramatic escapism from the realities of the war. In fact many people thought so, and few believed in it—but the few who did were people who mattered, and they included no less a person than the Premier of England, who at that moment was in a small room in Downing Street talking to a spare man of medium height, with wispy grey hair and keen grey eyes. From that worthy's drooping, humorous lips there hung a meerschaum pipe, and from the Premier's lips there jutted a cheroot, half-smoked.

A bull-like man, the Premier, with packed shoulders and a round, mobile face, showing even then something of the dynamic energy which moved in him.

"Well, now you know as much as I know, Craigie. I can't tell you anything else, but I want you to look into it. Get me a report as soon as you can, and give Smythe a ring when you want to see me."

"Ye-es," said Craigie, taking his pipe from his lips. "Have you half-an-hour to spare now?"

"Now?" Graham Hershall frowned.

"It's just on half-past seven," said Craigie, "and I've told two of my men to be at the office by twenty-five to eight. They might be able to tell us a little."

"What an amazing fellow you are, Craigie. I shall never quite get used to you. You heard nothing about this business until last night . . ."

6

Craigie smiled. "I knew something about it three months ago."

"*What?*"

"Three months," repeated Craigie.

"But—now that won't do," said Hershall almost sharply. "I should have had your report before now if that's the case."

If Craigie was worried by the rebuke he did not show it.

"There was nothing to report," he said, "and when I start send chits along to you based on suspicions and might-be's we'll stop getting on so well." Hershall gave an involuntary chuckle and stepped to the door. There was a twinkle in his heavily-lidded eyes as he opened it.

"I'll be ready in five minutes," he said.

Thus it happened that at twenty-five minutes to eight on that May evening, four people moved together towards an office in Whitehall. It could be approached from several directions, but that which Craigie and his men used most often was in a side-street, a small door which many passed by without noticing it.

It opened on to a narrow stone passage, which led to the cleaning and maintenance staff quarters in one direction, and in the other, to a flight of stone steps. The steps turned half-way up, on to a narrow landing. Here there were several press-buttons. None of them opened the door, but one showed a light inside the office and thus told Craigie that the caller knew his way about.

That evening Craigie pressed a button set in the staircase wall in a position where—he knew—only three other people could find it. As a result, what appeared to be a blank wall slid open, and showed his office, a long, low ceilinged room in one end of which was a large desk, a set of steel filing cabinets, and a Dictaphone.

The other end was a very different story. Four armchairs

were grouped round a fire, barely screening a large cupboard the half opened door of which disclosed a miscellany of homely objects.

The fire was burning brightly, the embers glowing red.

Craigie stepped aside for Hershall to enter, pushed a chair nearer the fire for the Premier, and poked the logs into a blaze. He had just finished when a light showed beneath the mantelshelf—a green light which glowed only for a moment and was accompanied by a faint buzzing sound.

Hershall's eyes crinkled at the corners.

"That's your man, I suppose? Who thought up all this ingenuity, Craigie?"

"I did," said Craigie, leaning forward and pressing another button. The sliding door opened to show the Errols.

Craigie solemnly introduced them. The grip of Hershall's hand was quick and firm. The Errols lowered themselves into the remaining armchairs and stretched out their long legs. The momentary embarrassment—if embarrassment it could be called—of finding a Prime Minster where none had been dreamt of, had quite gone.

"You would spring something on us like this," said Mike.

"Bibs and tuckers all creased," said Mark.

"Gentlemen," said Graham Hershall, "we are going to be serious, but I'll say first that the Air Force probably wishes it had many members like you. Now, I've just twenty minutes. You're going to start talking. Craigie?"

Craigie wasted no time.

"The Errols had best know first what you've told me," he said, and looked at the cousins. "Briefly, it is this: food supplies in England are being jeopardised by sabotage inside the country. We aren't seriously harassed by it yet, but unless it's stopped we may have real trouble."

Mike and Mark nodded but otherwise looked blank.

"A report on it has only just been presented to the Prime Minister," continued Craigie after a pause to light his pipe, "but we have known a little about it for three months. You two don't know it, but you have, in fact, been working on the affair."

"Good Lord! Are we provision merchants unknowingly?" queried Mike.

To a different man from Graham Hershall that remark might have seemed facetious enough to merit a rebuke. Hershall's eyes smiled however, and he puffed at his cheroot, the picture of a satisfied man—although in truth there were many things which did not satisfy him. Hershall knew these men; not the Errols personally, but the type which worked for Craigie. He knew many of their exploits, he knew above all things that there was not one of them who would hesitate to take enormous risks to carry out the orders of the mild-looking man who led them. And he had the wisdom to know that their facetious humour, although at times trying, carried them over many a difficult stretch. So he made no comment, and Craigie went on.

"The sabotage has been on a small scale. In fact for the first two months it looked as accidental as a run of bad luck. But when one or two underground food dumps were seriously damaged—the first occurred a month ago—it began to appear as organised sabotage. The Ministry of Food took it up, the Special Branch at the Yard worked on it . . ."

"No one thought it necessary to tell me," interposed the Prime Minister.

"And I heard whispers from half-a-dozen sources which made me give it some thought," continued Craigie mildly. "There was obviously one factor of importance—all of the trouble took place in the thirty-ninth food area."

"Sly beggar, isn't he, sir?" asked Mike Errol of the Prime

Minister. "All he told us was that someone was getting at the Commissioner for that area, and told us to look about us."

"Have you had any results," demanded Hershall sharply.

"They telephoned me this afternoon that they thought they had," said Craigie. "Which of you is going to tell this story—we'd rather have it in one piece."

"Oh, let them use their usual method," said Hershall easily.

Mike looked at Mark, who nodded. Mike said slowly:

"Sir Thomas Arkeld's the Commissioner, of course—middle-aged director of one or two multiple grocery firms, good man as far as we can see. Do you know him, sir?"

Hershall nodded.

"Good, that helps," said Mike. "He has one weakness, if it can be called that. The ladies. He's a bachelor, fair reputation—nothing underhanded, if you follow me, but . . ."

"I know him quite well enough to see what you mean," said Hershall. "Go on."

"Thanks. We checked up on his inamoratas. There are three at the moment—two he has known for many years, the other is a newcomer. Really a beauty, I could get enthusiastic . . ."

"Don't," said Mark drily

Hershall stopped a chuckle.

"Well, there she is," said Mike, his retrospective admiration unabated. "I'd say she's thirty, no more and perhaps a bit less. Dark. English, as far as we can judge. All the money she wants, judging from her dress, a flat in Town and a glorious little cottage in the country—we had a look over the cottage yesterday, she left for Town in the morning and Wally—one of our men, sir—followed her. No papers, no nothing there—we're talking confidentially, of course; we had no warrant or anything but . . ."

"Go on," said Hershall.

"Thanks. Right, then, the only thing to make us suspicious was that she's a new element, and could be working on Arkeld on whatever business Craigie had in mind—there was a good connection, that was pretty obvious. However," said Mike a little dreamily, "we weren't as clever as we thought. The lady didn't go straight to London, and surprised us while we were there. We had to push a tablecloth over her head to stop her from seeing us—and us from seeing her, quite a waste really. The cogent point being, of course, that she had managed to shake Wally off, and that meant that she was aware that she was under suspicion."

"Isn't that jumping to conclusions?" asked Hershall.

"The quickest way to reach 'em," said Mike instructively. "Thus we decided that she was suspicious of being suspected, and she wanted to find who was after her. It didn't mean she thought that it was Special Branch, or anything like that, of course—might have been a private worry for all we know. Supposing she has a husband? However, she managed a neat trick, and had us followed. A shrimpy little beggar was on our heels down from Bedford and we let him get as far as the flat before we nobbled him. He's at the flat now," added Mike offhandedly. "Wally's looking after him. But that isn't the worrying angle. We went to the Cherry—know it, sir?"

"It used to be a night club," said Hershall. "Yes."

"A tea-club now, near enough," said Mike. "Sad days! Anyhow, we went in for a drink. And who should be there but Arkeld's lovely lady, name of Myra, Myra Berne, if her identity card tells the truth. Odd spot, isn't it?"

2
SHRIMPY LITTLE MAN

There was an implied compliment in the fact that Hershall asked no questions, not even requesting any details that they may have omitted; he tacitly assumed that they had told all they knew, and he was right. There was silence in the office for some seconds, and then Hershall said:

"You propose to question this man, of course?"

"I expect Wally's on the job now," said Mike.

"Hmm. Well, I'll be glad to know what you find as soon as possible, but there's one thing, Craigie. It is a fact that all the trouble has been in the thirty-ninth area. Be frank. Do you suspect Arkeld?"

"I haven't reached the stage of suspecting anyone yet," said Craigie, "but I've one or two ideas."

"Let me have them."

"If it's Arkeld who is causing the trouble, I don't see much object in it. The country's divided into so many areas— running into hundreds, of course. A complete failure of supplies in any one area will cause no serious difficulty— nothing more, in fact, than a temporary dislocation. The obvious assumption is that the trouble is German-inspired, and Germany wouldn't waste time on one small area. *One* Commissioner might be approachable, even two or three—but there would be no possibility of a wholesale system of treachery amongst them."

"Quite right," Hershall nodded.

"So that it's more likely that others than the Commissioner are implicated," said Craigie, "and that the Director-General and Regional Directors might be vulnerable to some kind of approach."

Hershall cleared his throat.

"If you assume that Arkeld is vulnerable through this Berne woman, who gets information and passes it on, then someone may try to get it from the men who can do more extensive harm—*hmm.* Quite obvious, of course. What do you propose?"

Craigie smiled. "I've the five Directors under survey," he said, "and the reports should be in today or tomorrow. I thought you would like to hear the Errols' story, and . . ."

"And to know you were doing what could be done," said Hershall a trifle heavily. "Yes, I spoke too soon. But keep me in touch, Craigie. Good luck, Errols." He rose from his chair in sprightly fashion especially for so heavy a man, nodded, and stepped to the door. The Errols sprang to show him out, and Craigie pressed the control button.

"Don't let your ascetic appreciation of beauty grow too deep," said the Prime Minister to Mike Errol, and his lips parted in a quick smile before he walked swiftly down the stairs.

Once outside, they knew that he would be seen and followed by his Special Branch detectives, there was no need for them to worry about him. Mike pushed a hand through his hair.

"If that wasn't a dirty crack, I've never heard one."

"You asked for it," said Mark. "If I'd let you, you would have launched into a detailed description of her."

Craigie interrupted mildly:

"When you've finished, perhaps you'll tell me more about the business. I didn't know Wally was with you."

"Nor did we," said Mark. "He turned up—he'd been convalescing, hadn't he, and was with friends in Bedford. He saw us at a pub, and came in very useful. But what's worrying me is whether the girl followed us to the Cherry, or whether she was there by accident."

"You went by chance?" asked Craigie.

"We-ell," began Mike.

"Not quite," said Mark.

"It was more or less like this," said Mike. "We ran out of matches when we had a look-see at her cottage, and grabbed a book of them on a table. They happened to be issued by the Cherry Club, so we thought we'd look in—we are members, by the way."

"Mind you," said Mark, "we wouldn't have taken the chance if she'd seen us, but she didn't. Positively sure about that. We heard her car, and hid under the stairs until she came in, Mike with a tablecloth in hand waiting to jump out ghost-fashion and envelop her. She didn't have a chance of seeing us."

"Had she had any before?"

"Not much. Not enough to think we were after her."

"Have you talked to her?"

"Not yet," said Mike, regretfully.

Craigie's forehead wrinkled.

"It looks as if her visit to the Cherry was quite accidental. Someone ought to be there with her—why didn't you ring me?"

Mike grinned. "Someone was with her. Spats."

"That's all right then," said Gordon Craigie with a smile, "you'll be teaching me my business next. I'll send someone to support him, and you get to the flat and see Wally and the shrimp. Is there a definite connection between the shrimp and the woman?"

"Only that we watched her, and he was watching us. They could be nothing to do with each other."

"Doesn't seem too conclusive," said Craigie. "All right, then, off you go."

The Errols departed, hailed a taxi, and were driven to their flat in Brook Street.

They did not speak while in the cab.

They thought, nevertheless, of the good fortune which had sent Wally Davidson, one of Craigie's oldest agents, oldest, that was, in years of service—to Bedford, where he was able to help them. But for that they may have had some difficulty in trapping the shrimpy little man, who, they believed, was then being interrogated by Wally.

They thought also of Spats Thornton.

Thornton, too, was an agent of Craigie's, but he had not been detailed for work just then, and from their flat they had telephoned him. They had met him at the Cherry Club, but given no indication that they were old friends, and they had indicated the woman by the bar in a way which Thornton could not possibly have failed to understand. The occasional loud words from Mike Errol had not been purposeless: they had drawn Thornton's attention to the woman, and that would be enough.

Such ruses were now almost habitual.

They had been working for Craigie for a little over two years: in the beginning they had been green indeed, and prone to many mistakes, but they had learned quickly—particularly under the tutelage of one William Loftus, who was Craigie's leading agent. And as if by mental telepathy they thought of Loftus at the same time. Mike said:

"I wonder who . . ."

"Bill's after," finished Mark.

"Nice work!" grinned Mike. "He's probably on the tail of the Director-General. What's the chappy's name?"

"Sir Bruce Mortimer," said Mark.

"Hm-*hmm*. Bill's welcome to him."

The taxi came to a halt. Mark paid the fare, while Mike looked up and down Brook Street. There were few people about, probably because it was getting near dusk, and the streets cleared surprisingly quickly when darkness fell, even though the regularity of night warnings had not been maintained after the first few months of the Blitz.

"What are you gaping at?" Mark demanded as he turned from the cab and almost bumped into his cousin.

"I'm not gaping, I'm cogitating," said Mike in an injured tone. "I didn't think grey bowlers would ever be seen again off a race-course. Interesting features, too, I . . ."

"We are going to have no more of your descriptions tonight," declared Mark firmly, and he led Mike to the porch of the house.

He had nevertheless taken a full if concealed glance at the man in the grey bowler. A large man, a fat man with a red face, a gold chain spread over his mighty paunch, and black patent leather shoes atwinkle beneath.

Mark put a key in the door.

As he did so the fat man in the grey bowler moved, although they did not see him. They did not hear anything except a sound which might have been a sneeze from the other side of the road until there was a sharp noise close to Mike's head. He looked round, startled, to receive a shower of brick-dust and chippings in the face, causing a sudden sharp pain to his eyes. A bullet dropped from the wall to the garden paving.

"Get in!" he snapped.

He was afraid any moment that a second bullet would follow the first. In fact he was surprised that none did, although he was more immediately concerned with the pain which the brick-dust was causing to his eyes. He had his hands to his face, and consequently there was a sharp alarm in Mark's voice.

"What's happened?"

"It's all right," gasped Mike. "Bowler Hat, I think . . ."

Mark moved quickly.

He put one hand to his hip pocket and drew out a small automatic pistol. The man in the grey bowler was not immediately in sight. Mark peered up and down the road, and then he saw a thing which he could hardly believe.

The fat man was running.

Had Mark been asked his opinion, he would have said that the man could have managed nothing more than a shambling trot, but he would have been wrong. Bowler Hat ran well, on his toes, and at considerable speed. He was heading towards a large Daimler which was parked at one end of the street.

Mark fired.

The target might have seemed too big to miss, but miss he did, although a little spray of chippings from the pavement rose to one side of his quarry. He saw other chippings although he had fired only once, and he knew that someone was shooting at the fat man from the windows above.

That would be Wally Davidson.

It was as well that there were few people in Brook Street, for in a crowded thoroughfare the shooting would have caused much damage. As it was three people began to shout, and one had the daring to dart across the road towards the fugitive. A policeman joined him.

Neither man reached the fat man.

Mark saw them stop as they ran, saw the policeman fall forward, and the pedestrian stagger and slump to the ground. The shooting stopped. The fat man reached the Daimler, and the car started off, the speed of its getaway proving that there had been someone at the wheel.

A police whistle shrilled out as it turned into Piccadilly, but Mark Errol did not think there was much prospect of the car being caught. With mixed feelings he approached the second constable, and showed a card which stopped unnecessary questions. He waited until the ambulance arrived, and two casualties—neither badly hurt—were helped in.

The small crowd soon dispersed, and a very thoughtful Mark Errol walked back to the flat.

Wally Davidson let him in. He was tall, thin, and good looking, with an affectation of weariness by now so ingrained that it had become second nature.

"Hallo," he said. "Come in and join the party."

"How's Mike?" asked Mark quickly.

"He's all right. A bit of grit in his eyes, nothing more. We *are* having fun, aren't we?"

"Yes, aren't we," said Mark gruffly. "How have you been getting on?"

"Fairish," said Davidson. "Neither better nor worse."

As he spoke Mike came from the bathroom, dabbing a red and watery eye. He managed a wry grin.

"So the chap got away. How did you manage to miss him?"

"That's what I'm wondering," said Mark. "How long had he been there?"

"He arrived twenty minutes ago," said Davidson, and proceeded to explain his own course of action. He had talked with little effect to the shrimpy man—who, he said, was at that moment in the spare bedroom—and he had left the man for a while and looked out of the window. He had seen the grey-bowlered man arrive, and not liking the cut of his bowler, decided to keep an eye on him.

When the Errols had arrived, the fat man had moved his hand to his coat pocket. He had fired through his coat, Wally said, but only once, for Wally had returned the fire quickly and the fat man had taken to his heels.

"And that," declared Wally, stifling a yawn, "is all I can tell you. I'm damned annoyed, all the same—I could have sworn I punctured his hide twice."

"You hit the pavement once or twice," said Mark glumly. "We would miss something as large as that, wouldn't we? Oh, well, we'll report to Gordon when we've had another shot at Shrimpy. He's not talkative, you say?"

"We misnamed him," said Davidson. "He's a clam."

"I'll prise him open," said Mark.

There was little doubt that he had been really afraid that Mike had been hit in the face, and that the fear had worried him: moreover, the failure to stop the fat man was—and for some time would continue to be—on his mind. So far it was quite impossible to see ahead, or even to understand the movements of the fat man beyond the bare essential that he had wanted the Errols dead. But one thing was certain; his escape laid up a store of trouble for the Department.

Craigie would not blame them for it; Craigie never apportioned blame except for negligence. But the fact remained, and its effect was more obvious on Mark Errol than on the others.

Davidson, in fact, seemed in good humour.

"You wouldn't believe what our little clam has for a voice," he said. "It's . . ."

"I thought you said he hadn't talked," and Mark sharply.

"Good heavens, Mark, how pedantic can you get! What I *should* have said had I known you to be in a professor mood was, he hadn't given any information. Now listen."

He stepped with exaggerated stealth to the door of the spare room, and called:

"Are you ready yet?"

For a moment there was no answer; in fact the moment was so prolonged that in Mark Errol's mind there jumped the fear that the shrimp of a man was no longer a prisoner. And then the voice came.

"Get to hell wid you."

The words, of course, did not explain the starts of surprise registered on the faces of the Errols. It was the voice that was all important. Deep, sonorous, low-pitched, it might have come from a giant.

"Uncanny, isn't it," said Wally. "Shall we go in?"

Mark said uneasily: "I wish Bill were here."

"Well, he isn't," said Davidson. He said it regretfully, for all of them would gladly have seen Bill Loftus, would as gladly have left him to deal with the recalcitrant prisoner.

Davidson unlocked the door. It was a fact that the effect of the deep voice was such that all of them half-expected some kind of sensation, but they were disappointed. Sitting back in an easy chair in the small spare room was the little shrimp of a man. He was ordinary to a degree. His face was neither ugly nor handsome; nor were his physical characteristics in any way out of the ordinary.

He looked at the oncoming three, his expression one of insolence touched with bravado.

"Can't yer do it on yer own?" he demanded of Davidson.

The sepulchral voice would have reduced them to laughter in different circumstances; Mark was half inclined to tell the man to stop fooling. But there could surely be no purpose in such a masquerade; it must be natural.

Mark stood squarely in front of the prisoner. He did not immediately speak, and his expression was calculated to inspire nervousness. It succeeded, up to a point.

"You followed me from Bedford to London," Mark said evenly. "Why?"

"Becawse I liked the sight o' yer behind," said the Shrimp promptly, and with a grin that showed a surprisingly good set of teeth.

The grin disappeared a moment later, for Mark struck him with the palm of his hand. It was the kind of thing that most of Craigie's men had to do from time to time; nothing brought information more quickly than a show of violence and a threat of something more.

The trio expected a spate of abuse, but they had made a mistake, for the Shrimp moved.

It seemed impossible; no one *should* have been able to move like that from his position. But the Shrimp did so, hurtling all his weight at Mark Errol, who was taken both by surprise and by the force of the leap. He staggered backwards, and the little man clung to him, getting his fingers tight about Mark's throat.

3

NOT A GOOD DAY

For the Errols it was not a good day.

There was little time for thinking, but in the moments at Mark's disposal he was aware of a fear that he was about to die. It was not only the way his breath had been knocked from his body; it was the tight grip on his throat, one so skilfully applied that the thumb pressed hard into his windpipe and he could not draw a breath. His head filled with a strange humming and his lungs reached bursting point—he was so nearly unconscious in a matter of seconds that he was not immediately aware that Mike and Wally had prised the Shrimp's hand away.

"It's all right, Mark. We've got him."

The little man had slumped, as if he accepted the fact that he had no chance to get away from the three of them. He allowed himself to be pushed back into his chair without making any effort at self-defence. Mark's head cleared, and he sat up; his recovery was expedited by a weak whisky-and-soda which Mike prepared. In perplexity he contemplated the man who had so nearly strangled him.

It would have been easy enough to beat him up, but violence for the sake of it was not in his mind. They wanted the man to talk, and they needed to find a way of doing it. It did not look as if violence was the required method.

"Stalemate," murmured Mike.

"If that means yer stuck, it's right first time," said the cavernous voice unexpectedly. "Like I told longshanks 'ere, I don't talk, see. Not to you, or the ruddy narks, or anyone, see. Wotjer think yer going ter do wiv' me now I'm 'ere?"

"We haven't quite decided," said Wally, "but we will." He nodded to the Errols. They all went out, and as Wally locked the door he smiled gloomily.

"Round two to the shrimp, I think."

"Why two?" asked Mike.

"You forget I've already had a go at him. I threatened him all I could think of, and Bill couldn't have done it better, but he kept his mouth closed on everything that mattered. I wish . . ."

"Bill were here, I know," growled Mark. "Great Scott, are we going to let a little runt like that beat us? There must be some way of making him talk."

"We could give him a sleeping draught, and see if he talks in his sleep," said Mike.

Mark looked at him coldly.

"Don't be an idiot. Oh, well, one of us ought to report to Craigie."

Davidson reached for his hat. "I suppose it had better be me. Watch the little blighter while I'm gone. I wouldn't be surprised if he's a trick or two in his locker."

"That struck me," said Mike.

The others eyed him, and he went on slowly:

"Damn it, he wouldn't be so cocksure if he thought he was going to be here long. He must think he'll be released. I wonder if he expects the fat man?"

Something akin to excitement showed in Mark's and Wally's eyes, and together they said:

"You've got it."

Mike said a trifle smugly: "I do believe I have. All right, he expects the fat one will get him out, and he doesn't know that the fat one has been and tried and gone. Shall we try again from that angle?"

"No-o," Wally demurred. "Give him half-an-hour—until I'm back," he added ingenuously. "He'll be worried because time's dragging. Haven't *either* of you any idea why he followed you?"

"It could only be because we were watching the woman."

"Hmm. The watcher watched. Oh, well," said Davidson. "I'll get back as soon as I can."

He went out, looking cautiously up and down the street; but dusk was gathering, and it was impossible to see clearly for more than fifty yards. Nothing untoward happened, however, and he reached Whitehall without interference. Thus he was able to report to Craigie that from appearances he judged that the flat was no longer being watched. He made a full statement of the other developments, and as he expected Craigie lost no time in vain regrets.

"Get back to the flat," he said easily, "and make sure that you keep our Shrimp. I'll send Bill over as soon as I can."

"Will he be long?"

"He phoned from Guildford that he hopes to be back in three or four hours," said Craigie.

"Oh, well," Davidson said, "if we've got to wait we've got to. Is he on to something?"

"I earnestly hope so," said Craigie.

As Davidson went out, he wondered what was in Craigie's mind. That it held danger and risk he knew, aware as were all

Craigie's men that their lives were so close to death that it had, in fact, become a close familiar.

Next to Craigie, Loftus was the most important of the Department men; the difference being that Craigie had the capacity for detailed organisation, while Loftus's mind worked better when he was in action. He moved faster than Craigie when on a job, but between jobs his mind went, as it were, moribund. At all times Craigie would be taken for what he was: a clever, deep thinking man. But when Loftus was not working he gave the impression that he was a fool; and indeed he often acted like one.

Davidson again decided that the quicker Loftus arrived the better. Crossing St. James's Park, he became aware that he was being followed.

He would not have noticed it but for a peculiar fact.

The black-out was complete and the night was pitch dark, without a moon, and with the stars hidden by heavy clouds, but as he had turned into the park a car's headlights had shone on a diminutive creature in a bright red beret.

Davidson had thought, when he had first seen her, that it was criminal to allow a child to be out after dark, with London as it was, but he had stopped himself from questioning her. He was glad of that when he saw her illuminated again in the lights of another car. There was no mistaking the bright red beret, and the pale, thin face of the child.

But she was older than he had first thought.

There was, of course, the possibility that she had followed him for the sake of company, and so he walked the length of Piccadilly, strolled about the Circus, and then walked back on the other side. There was very little traffic, but three times he saw the red beret and the pinched, childish face.

Did she want to beg from him?

Deliberately he stopped at a tobacconist's, buying cigarettes he did not want. When he came out, the girl was waiting, and as he walked on again, continued to follow him.

Davidson scowled in the darkness.

He had given her the opportunity of begging, or of asking the way, and she had neglected it. She could only be following him with an ulterior motive. She was not old enough for the streets—or he hoped not—and even had she been, that would hardly have explained her silent, faithful shadowing.

Could the fat man be using a child for a trailer?

It was a problem which worried Davidson. How did one deal with a child?

He hesitated outside the flat, and then went in.

Five minutes afterwards he came out again, and saw her standing quite still, close to the rails.

She was two yards away from him when he stepped forward.

"Now what's all this?" he demanded, and he could not make his voice sound anything less than kindly. She was such a mite, and the darkness showed him no more than the blur of her pale face.

She did not answer. Davidson frowned.

"Is there anything you want?"

He put his hand out, but she shrank away.

"This won't do, you know," he said, hoping he didn't look as big a fool as he felt.

He wished he could see her face plainly, but that was impossible.

He tried again.

"Are you hungry?" he asked, and for the first time she spoke, but not to answer his question.

"My—my Daddy went in there."

"What?" demanded Wallace Davidson blankly.

"Yes, he did," she said, and she had a sweet, attractive voice. "I saw him go there."

"When was this?" demanded Davidson.

"A long time ago," she said, and with the ice once broken she appeared to have found confidence in him, for a small hand stretched up and reached his. "Everso long. Nearly tea-time."

"Oh," said Davidson. "And did you have any tea?"

"No."

"Did you have any supper?"

"No-o," she said a little hesitantly.

"I see," said Davidson. "Well, let's get in, shall we, and see if we can find some supper and also your Daddy. Does he work here?" he added as she stepped trustfully with him into the house.

"Oh, *no,*" she said, "he works all over the place. He doesn't come home much, you see. Mummy and him aren't very good friends." This information, spoken so simply, caught at Davidson's heart.

"Yes?" he prompted her, as they reached the faintly lighted hallway.

"Well, sometimes he gives me a shilling, or even a half-crown," she said, "so if I see him I always wait for him, you see."

"Ye-es," said Davidson. "But why did you follow me?"

"I thought you might know where he was," she said.

"Then why not ask me?"

"I got frightened," she murmured. "I thought you might be cross."

"I see," said Davidson.

It had dawned on him some time before that the child's father was the Shrimp, but the belief did nothing to help him. How was he going to handle the situation when he reached the flat? He smiled somewhat grimly at the thought that here was a problem which would surely be beyond Loftus, and then he inserted his key into the door, urging her forward.

She hesitated a little, blinking in the stronger light of the front room, in which the Errols were busily at work on an impromptu meal. On the table were three bottles of beer, one unopened. A place was set for Wally.

The Errols glanced Davidson's way. Davidson had the impression that they were suddenly so still that they might have been carved from wood or stone. The child eyed them with obvious concern. At last Mark said gravely: "Hallo."

Both pairs of Errol eyes turned towards Davidson.

"She got lost, and . . ."

"No, I didn't get lost," the girl corrected him eagerly. "I saw my Daddy, and he came into this house. But he isn't either of these gentlemen."

"Well, that's something," said Mike.

Davidson watched the child take off her beret, scarf and coat, all of which she placed neatly on a chair. She could be no more than ten or eleven, he thought, but she had the poise of a young woman.

As he drew a chair up to the table for her, he wondered whether he could be wrong, and that the Shrimp was not her father. He was thinking how best to introduce the subject—at the middle or the end of the meal, which the child was eating with obvious enjoyment—when from the bedroom there came the cavernous voice:

"What erbout bringing me a drink?"

The girl started, and her face suddenly grew sharp and severe. It seemed to Davidson that there was unspoken accusation in her eyes—as if she were blaming him because he must have known someone else was in the flat.

She said: "That's my Daddy's voice."

"Oh, is it," said Wally, and he pushed his chair back. "He's staying with us for a little while, I think . . ." he looked at the Errols, who nodded their agreement to an unspoken query, and then went on: "But I could let you see him, if you want to."

"Yes, please," she said, trustful again. "He goes to all kinds of strange places, I know."

Mike Errol hid a grin as he unlocked the door, the child just behind him. The Shrimp did not immediately see her.

Then the man's wide mouth opened in surprise, and his little eyes narrowed so that they were scarcely visible. The child stared at him calmly.

"Hallo, Daddy. Didn't you see me this afternoon?"

"I—I don't remember," said the Shrimp.

The whole episode was so unusual, so innocent that when the little man stepped towards the door, Davidson did not stop him from entering the larger room. For once, no conceivable danger could be threatened.

The danger came from the child.

As her father—if the man *was* her father—moved forward, she skipped aside, much as a child would do from someone of whom she was afraid. She reached the door, and from the chair on which she had folded her coat and scarf *she took a small automatic pistol.* She held it steadily, pointing it towards Davidson and the Errols, while the Shrimp stepped towards her.

He was smiling, but with no appearance of amusement.

"Well, that's gotcher," he said and his voice echoed about the room incredibly low. "Thought you was clever, all of yer, but—gimme that gun, Topsy."

He took the gun from her, and the Errols knew that he meant to shoot for they read murder in his eyes.

4
ENTER LOFTUS

I t was a bad moment.

Not one of them had dreamed of this development, not one had suspected that behind the thin, pretty face of the child there could have lingered such cunning and trickery.

At least one of them would get hurt.

It was a recognisable rule in such a situation that all of them should go for their guns, and always at the same moment, determined by the first word any of them spoke.

The little man himself was now speaking with a sneer. "Like ter know why I follered yer. Well, lemme tell yer this—I follered becawse I never wanted yer to stick yer noses in anyone else's business, see, *and* I ain't gointer take any chances. I'll teach yer!"

There was a pause, and then:

"Will you?" asked Davidson.

Three things happened at once, or so quickly upon one another that there was no noticeable time-lag.

The Shrimp fired.

The trio moved towards their guns, in their hip-pockets.

And the door opened.

Asked afterwards, none of the trio could say which had really happened first, the shooting or the opening of the door; but it was logical to assume that the door had the honour, for it knocked against the gunman's back and spoiled his aim. Even then a bullet whizzed between the Errols, and each man felt the wind of it. The Shrimp swore, and swung round in an attempt to shoot at the interrupter: but a hand shot out and gripped his wrist. The gun dropped.

Like lighting Topsy ducked beneath the large man's arm.

She was so small and thin that she did this easily enough, moving with a speed which was really startling. It was Mark Errol who recovered first, rushed past the newcomer to the door and thundered downstairs.

When he reached the street he was greeted by two things; the pitch darkness of the night, and the first wail of the sirens. He could hear nothing, for the girl ran silently, and he had no idea which way she had gone.

The Shrimp found himself flat on the floor, looking up at a large man with an expression which certainly did not indicate any degree of affection. Ignoring him, the large man looked round at Mark, his lips curving into a smile.

"Now we're all together," he said pleasantly, "what's it all about?"

"You tell it," said Mark to Mike.

"Your turn," said Mike promptly. "I told the P.M."

"Wally shall talk," declared the large man with the air of one who had arbitrated in such decisions many times before.

Davidson grimaced and took out his cigarette case.

"Bill," he said, "we're glad to see you, but you're an hour or so too late."

"Well, really," said William Loftus amiably. "You do

surprise me. It looked to me as if I were just in time. Midgets flying through the air, little men letting off pistols."

He turned to the man on the floor, bent over him, and there followed the click of handcuffs. He took a handkerchief out next, and made it into an effective gag, while Mike Errol—after a hurried trip into the bedroom—came out with a small roll of cotton wool, which Loftus packed over the Shrimp's ears. That done, he picked the man up and dropped him on to a couch, sat himself in an easy chair and began to fill his pipe.

He was a large man, six-feet four and broad in proportion, with packed shoulders and a depth of chest which was awe-inspiring. He did not look overtly intelligent, and this fact, in the dangerous work which he undertook, could, by lulling his opponents to a state of false security, be a distinct advantage.

The Errols, looking at him with the eyes of affection and respect, saw that his clothes bore the look of having been slept in for several nights, that he needed a shave, and that he looked tired.

Loftus met their look of concern with a smile. It was a transforming thing, robbing his face of all suggestion of dullness, bearing instead a vitality and animation, that inspired either confidence or fear, according to the degree of friendship towards him.

Davidson was nearing the end of his narrative.

"Well, I ask you, what else could I do? She was only a kid, and she looked both nervous and hungry. I would have staked a fiver on her story being genuine."

"She took us all in," said Mike Errol.

"Well, there isn't much more," Davidson went on: "I thought it might be an idea if we let the—er—father see her, and so we opened the door. She dodged away and grabbed her gun."

"Quite a circus," said William Loftus. He yawned. "Sorry,

chaps, but I can't do anything before I have a sleep. I'm so dog-tired I feel I shall hit the floor at any minute. I've phoned Gordon, and the general idea is that we all stay here together. Thornton and Carry are looking after Mike's lady friend, and this and that has also been arranged."

"What about Sir Bruce Mortimer?" asked Mike.

"The Director-General of Food Conservation is in deep consultation with people of importance," said Loftus, "and he's not likely to leave London for twenty-four hours. I'll get along to my flat, I think, Ned ought to be there by now."

"What about this?" demanded Wally, looking at the prisoner.

"For the moment it can't hear a noise or make one. We'll leave it that way until morning. It might persuade him to loosen up." He rose, stretched, yawned, and smiled about him. "Yes, *quite* a circus you've been having."

Wally went down to the street door with him. His flat was a hundred yards along the street, at 55g, and he was there almost as soon as Wally was back with the Errols.

Ned Oundle, another of the Department agents, and Loftus's closest friend, rose to greet him. He was tall and thin with an air of childlike, but deceptive, innocence.

"Hallo, Bill. You look all in."

"I am all in, and in two minutes flat I shall, I hope, be tucked up in bed."

Ned Oundle followed him to his bedroom.

"Nothing to report?"

"Well, that's something. Heard anything of a lovely called Berne—Myra Berne?"

"Not a thing."

"Pity," said Loftus, flinging clothes to right and left. "Thornton and Carruthers are trying to get something on her.

They may ring through, but don't wake me unless it really won't keep."

He pulled on his pyjamas, slid between the sheets and, to all appearances, was asleep before Oundle put out the light. The thin man stood staring at his friend for a moment, a worried expression in his eyes. Loftus would not have been as tired as that without some very good cause—and if he had needed to work for so long without sleep, then there was serious trouble brewing.

Undoubtedly she was lovely. She was dressed in a dark green evening gown, and that made her unusual, for evening gowns were rarely worn in London those nights. Since being at the cocktail bar of the Cherry Club she had been to her Westminster flat, and changed.

Outside the flat two men were waiting—Thornton and Carruthers, Craigie's men. They cursed the black-out because they could see so little, but by arrangement with the hall porter of the block, Spats—a nickname earned by his initials—Thornton had a seat in his office, while Carruthers consoled himself as best he could in the darkness outside.

A man had entered the foyer.

He had walked straight to the lift and gone up, but the hall porter, who believed he was helping a private detective, nodded towards Thornton, an unspoken "that's him". Thornton had a vivid mind-picture of a tall, heavy-jowled man with a prominent nose—a man who would not easily be forgotten.

This man went to Myra Berne's flat, and neither rang nor knocked. Like her, he was in evening-dress. Inside the small hall of the flat he took off his silk scarf and his overcoat. The woman called to him:

"Is that you, Max?"

"Yes, my dear." His voice had a metallic timbre but was not otherwise unpleasant. "How long have you been here?"

"An hour or more."

"I see." He pushed open the lounge door, and went in. The room was furnished conventionally and luxuriously. There were many such interiors owned by those who could afford them.

The woman reclined on an over-cushioned settee, the lighting effect showing up her lovely face, her great green-grey eyes, and the smoothness of her skin.

Maximilian Golt stood quite still for some seconds, and then his heavy-jowled face broke into a smile. But there was nothing in his smile which had the transfiguring effect of Loftus's. It showed pleasure, perhaps a touch of lust; but it was confined to his lips.

Beauty, Mike Errol would have said, and the Beast. The description, though trite, was apt, for there was a touch of uncouthness about the man which civilised garb could not wholly disguise.

"And you contrived it safely?" he said.

"I think so. Come and sit down."

Ignoring her invitation, he took a quick step towards her, his eyes harsh and dangerous.

"You *think* so. What does that mean?"

She smiled and shrugged.

He stuck doggedly to the point. "Why only 'think'?"

"Because I'm not sure," she said. "Please don't lash about the room in that disquieting way. Drinks are where they always are, and I've ordered dinner. It will be up in a quarter of an hour."

He glared at her, and his lips tightened, but before he spoke again he opened a cocktail cabinet, took out whisky and soda and poured himself a drink. Her teeth, very fine and white, showed in a vaguely malicious smile.

"Aren't you going to ask me to join you?"

He drew a sharp breath, but his first drink had loosened his tongue and he spoke roughly.

"This isn't a game, you know. If you were followed from Bedford that's going to mean trouble . . ."

"It *might* mean trouble," she corrected.

He handed her a drink so sharply that it nearly spilled over her gown. The accident was averted, but the little incident appeared to worry her more than anything else had done, and there was a sharp note in her voice.

"Now listen to me, Max. We've been working for three months, and this is the first time anything has even looked like going wrong—we can't expect miracles. And we've practically finished with Arkeld, anyhow. Skippy told me that there was something the matter in Bedford—I was being followed."

Golt drank again, but said nothing.

"So I made arrangements to leave for London, and then doubled back to the cottage. Someone was there. I didn't see them, but on the other hand they didn't see Skippy. He kept them in sight all the time."

"And then?"

"I came down here," she said. "I don't think I was followed after that—there was a tall man who showed some interest but I think it was strictly personal." She laughed lightly. "In its way it was quite an adventure."

"You think so? Where's Skippy?"

"He hasn't reported yet."

"What time did you reach London?"

"About half-past six."

"What did you do?"

"I went to the Cherry. Max, is this catechism necessary?"

"I think so, yes." His voice struck a harsh, metallic note. "How long did you stay there?"

"An hour."

"Was anyone there?"

"None of our people. The place was practically deserted."

"So you got to London at half-past six, and Skippy hasn't reported yet? When did you last see him?"

"At the cottage."

"You stayed there too long," he said, and he began to pace the room. "What I want to know is who followed you—were they the police?"

"Skippy says they weren't the type."

"What does he know about it! Where's Arkeld?"

"He came to London yesterday," she said. "He's getting quite a bore, darling, don't you think we can get on to someone else?"

"There weren't any papers at the cottage, were there?"

"Don't be a fool."

"And don't get too quick with your answers," he snapped. "I don't like this business, and if Skippy doesn't turn up soon there'll be cause enough for worry. You're ready to move at any time?"

She tightened her lips.

"I don't want . . ."

"I don't give a damn what you want. If you're suspected then you're leaving here *and* the cottage, and no arguing. There's enough trouble as it is. Someone's watching Mortimer—I can't make out who it is, but he's a clever beggar. There could be a connection between him and our men, but I hope to God there isn't. The Special Branch never leave off once they get their teeth into a job."

"I—see," said Myra softly. "So you've come a cropper. I think . . ."

What she thought did not transpire then, for there was a sharp ringing at the doorbell. Golt hesitated, turned off the light, and opened the door. As he stood there in the half light a diminutive creature slipped past him.

Davidson and the Errols would have recognised "Topsy."

5

TOPSY TALKS

The "child's" red beret and dark blue mackintosh, and her general air of poverty and pallor, made an odd contrast in the luxurious room. But she moved to the fire as if she was used to it. Holding her hands to the blaze, she said sharply:

"They've got Skippy."

The effect was devastating. Myra, her poise already a little disturbed, sat bolt upright. Golt swore; it was not a pleasant sound.

"Who's 'they'?" he demanded thickly.

Clearly and concisely the "child" explained what had happened, then moving to the cocktail cabinet began to mix herself a gin-and-Italian.

"Whose place did he go into?" rapped Golt.

She described Mark and Michael Errol quickly and graphically, but neither the woman nor Golt recognised them from the description. "They're the man-about town type," she went on, "but they're used to trouble all right, and so is the big lout."

Golt said sharply: "Who?"

"The one who stopped me from getting Skippy away," she said. "I haven't seen a bigger man for years."

"*My God!*" said Golt harshly, "it sounds like the man who is watching Mortimer!" He gave a brief word-picture of Loftus, and the sharp eyes of the "child" narrowed. When he finished she nodded.

"That's him, all right."

"So they *are* on to Mortimer as well as you," Golt said roughly to Myra. "The police . . ."

"They aren't police," said Topsy sharply.

"Oh, aren't they? And who gave you that private information?"

"I just know," Topsy snapped. "And don't vent your rage on me."

For a moment it looked as if Golt would strike her, but if that had been his intention it was quelled by the arrival of the waiter with dinner. Topsy left soon afterwards and the man and the woman were alone again.

They ate in silence. When the telephone bell shrilled through the room, Golt leapt to answer it.

He listened with tightened lips, then banged the receiver down violently.

"That was Barker. He tried to get these Errol people—he was watching Skippy at the same time—but they made him run for it. He doesn't like it any more than I do." He drummed his fingers for a moment and then appeared to come to a decision. "I'm going to see Kay."

"Without an appointment?"

"I don't have to have one for emergency, and this is an emergency all right. I'm going to tell him you're trying to get a line on these Errols. Make what inquiries you can, and find out where they're likely to be." He leered. "One of them might be susceptible."

Without another word he picked up his hat and scarf, and went out.

Myra sat for a moment gazing into the fire, her face expressionless. Then she shrugged her shoulders, and rang for a taxi. Slipping into a fur coat she went downstairs.

When she had passed the hall porter's box, Thornton followed her.

Already Carruthers had followed Maximilian Golt, although that task might easily prove futile in the black-out. This might be easier, for the woman had phoned for a cab and Thornton had been able to arrange for another to be waiting for him. Once started, the driver seemed to have no difficulty in keeping his quarry in sight.

Golt's private car, meanwhile, went on towards a house in the Regent's Park area. He drove well and carefully, and the journey took him twenty-five minutes. He did not leave the car in the street but took it to a small garage nearby, where a night-mechanic was on duty. Then he walked back to the house, walking slowly up the steps leading to the front door.

He seemed afraid.

Twice he hesitated when he reached the door, but finally he pressed the bell sharply. There was a pause before the door was opened.

As the crack widened, Golt stepped through.

He saw a middle-aged man with snow-white hair cropped close. Apart from that fact, he was nondescript enough.

"Have you an appointment, sir?"

"No. The matter is urgent."

"I will see if Mr. Kay is free, sir."

The man mounted a wide staircase and disappeared round the bend in a landing. The landing was large, its entire walls, as those of the hall, hung with portraits. If there was anything surprising about them it was that they were all of men; they were also valuable.

Golt, however, was not interested in portraits; he paced the floor impatiently, momentarily blind to the charm of the Sheraton pieces with which the hall was furnished, and the air of luxury and age which was in it.

He glanced repeatedly up the staircase.

Once a door opened and he heard the strains of music, and a gentle voice, sweet but untrained, perhaps that of a young girl. The door closed and the sound was cut off. A voice said:

"Good evening. Can I help you?"

Golt turned abruptly. The floor was thickly carpeted and thus had muffled the sound of footsteps. He looked into the pleasant, fresh-coloured face of a youngish man, whose brown hair was curly and whose hazel eyes held a look of faint interrogation.

"No, thanks," Golt said. "I've seen someone."

The young man smiled and went on up the stairs. He was of medium height, and lithe, although his shoulders were broad and powerful. Golt hardly remembered what he looked like, but it passed through his mind that it was another of the young fools Kay employed.

Footsteps again, and the servant returned.

"If you will wait for a few minutes, sir, Mr. Kay will see you."

Golt opened his lips to protest that the matter was urgent, but knew it was useless. One could never hurry Kay, and it was not wise to question what he did and said. Golt disliked that fact particularly, since he himself had been used to giving orders and having them obeyed without argument.

After ten minutes, the servant came again, and took him upstairs. From the room to which he was being led the young man appeared and passed him, nodding briefly. So he had been to see Kay—it was like the man to keep him waiting while he had word with a young secretary.

Golt entered the study, a room he had seen several times before, and which had at first impressed him by its opulence, and the Oriental manner of its furnishing.

The lighting was cleverly arranged by reflection, showing no lamps. It spread a palish lemon glow about the dark-painted ceiling and the draperies, and it gave to the man sitting at the ornately-carved desk a peculiar yellowness.

Golt never failed to be startled when he saw the man he knew as Kay.

He had not seen him in any place but this room, nor in any posture but sitting at the desk. He appeared to be immensely old, yet Golt had come to the conclusion that "old" was the wrong word: "ageless" was better.

Dark eyes watched him now, eyes which seemed not to move.

Above them the brows were well-marked, and quite white, as was the Van Dyke beard and the hair, the bleached effect accentuated by the wearing of a black fez. The fez gave a greater impression of height to his forehead, of contrast in light and shade.

Black—and white: that was Kay—for his skin, too, was of that colourless texture sometimes seen in albinos.

His voice was strangely out of keeping, strong and firm, cultured but in no way unusual. He addressed Golt. "Were you followed?"

"No," said Golt.

But he was not sure, and he was afraid the other would know that. Kay always put him at a disadvantage, always took control of the situation. Golt tried to emulate him when with others, but it rarely worked; Myra was never impressed, nor Topsy—or for that matter Skippy and Barker.

"Why have you come?"

Golt, who had rehearsed his story half-a-dozen times, was suddenly unable to find words. The silence deepened, but the man at the desk seemed to be possessed with the patience of Job; he would do nothing to help the other out. Golt started at last; but as he continued, and as he dwelt on the carelessness of Myra, Skippy and others, he grew more confident. He was at pains to show that he was in no way to blame.

Kay made no comment on that, but asked:

"The large man. Describe him."

Golt did so.

"And you do not know his name?"

"No, not yet. But I'll find it, don't worry. I thought I'd better tell you just how things are, we don't want a slip-up now, do we?"

"We are not going to have a slip-up," said Kay quietly. "I can tell you the name of the large man. It is Loftus."

Golt stared. "*Loftus?* How did you know?"

"In a matter of this kind, Golt, it is necessary to have the measure of all possible opposition. I was quite aware that we might sooner or later be compelled to cross swords with the Department—Department Z, they call it; there is something childish in the minds of bureaucrats, Golt, they give a Department a letter instead of a name, and thus surround it with an aura of mystery, with the result that no one believes in it. However, Loftus is the man. He is the leading light in this Department, and as you appear to have realized, he is dangerous."

"How he got on to us beats me," said Golt.

"It would, and it *is* disturbing, but . . ." Kay shrugged. "I think it is clear at long last that all the trouble has been in Arkeld's particular area. So Arkeld is watched, and thus it would be easy for them to see in Myra Berne a possible leakage of information. That is the A B C of such investigations. We are lucky that they did not get acquainted with Arkeld and Myra until the gentleman's area had been satisfactorily covered. The first part has been carried out well, Golt, but there is much to be done."

"You don't have to tell me that," muttered Golt.

"That is good. I thought that you perhaps considered that we had done enough." There was a hint of menace in the words. Golt licked his lips, and looked away from the strange dark eyes of the man he knew as Kay.

"At the moment I am a little concerned with Loftus's personal interest in Mortimer," continued Kay. "We shall have to prevent that. Mortimer is very valuable—although, of course, he has no idea of that!" Kay widened his lips in a silent laugh, strangely uncanny. "However, all this is by the way. Now—you feel it wise to get your man Skippy away at all costs?"

"That's right, I do."

"Two attempts have failed—how much does he know?"

"He could blow *my* part of it," said Golt gruffly.

"All of it?"

"If they get the low-down on him they'll get us all—my people, I mean."

"Ye-es. That is possible. However, we could prevent that catastrophe in more ways than one. Have you any particular affection for—er—Skippy?"

"What are you driving at?" queried Golt, uneasily.

"The possibility of preventing him from talking," said Kay suavely. "It will be much easier than physical attacks on Loftus and the others—until you know the Department you cannot realise how difficult they can make a situation. A lot of young men work for Loftus and his leader, Craigie. They must be circumvented of course. But I don't particularly want the hue and cry that would follow the murder of any one of them. It would do no good. I would much rather have Loftus and his friends very busily engaged in barking up the wrong tree, while I am happily pushing forward my own project. I will work something out, and you will think of a means of disposing of Skippy."

Golt licked his lips.

"He's pretty useful . . ."

"Not any more. They know him. He is now not only useless but dangerous. If he should get away we must have nothing more to do with him. The other way will be easier. All right, Golt, arrange it. And—what of Myra?"

"I've told her to get a line on these Errol fellows."

For some seconds there was silence, and then Kay nodded very slowly.

"Yes, that might well prove useful." Again came that silent laughter. "All right, Golt. Do not get in touch with me unless I send for you, and when you do come be sure it is after dark."

"I'm not a fool," said Golt irritably.

"I trust not," said Kay pleasantly.

But when the door had closed behind Golt he lifted a telephone. His voice came sharp and clear.

"Follow Golt, and see if he is alone."

It was half-an-hour later that the telephone rang, and he was assured that no one had been on Golt's heels. For some minutes Kay sat brooding, with his eyes closed. There was no expression on his pallid face. Then suddenly he stood up.

He was surprisingly short; so short that any man seeing his head and shoulders and chest would have been startled, for his legs were under-developed in size, although they carried him surely enough. He made a grotesque appearance as he stepped to the door, opened it, and then walked quickly downstairs.

He passed no one.

He reached the room from which Golt had heard strains of music. A girl was softly playing on a Beckstein grand. A young man—the same one who had spoken to Golt—leaned against the piano watching her.

It was a light and lovely thing, a Chopin mazurka, and she played with feeling and a sureness of touch which would have given any Chopin-lover pleasure. She did not see the door open, and looked up with a start when Kay approached.

Her hands left the keys immediately, and the young man straightened up.

"No, go on, go on," said Kay gently. "I came to hear you play, my dear, I have to compose my thoughts, and nothing encourages and soothes me more. Perhaps you could sing— just a little. Charles, bring me that chair up, will you?"

The secretary obeyed, the girl played and sometimes sang, and the man called Kay leaned back with his eyes closed and his fingers interlaced, his absurdly short legs tucked beneath him.

Who could have guessed that he was planning murder?

6

SHOCKS FOR CRAIGIE

Loftus lay on his back, snoring gently. A patch of sun shining on the wall just touched the tip of his nose. One arm was flung over the coverlet, the other was snug inside the bed.

Oundle opened the door.

Theirs was a service flat, and next door to it was another—with a communicating door—where Diana Woodward, Loftus's fianceé, stayed when she was in London. At the moment she was in America, and Loftus was afraid that she was likely to remain there until the war was over. The knowledge that she was at least safe from bombing attacks was no great comfort, for her work was as hazardous as his, and it was worrying to know that she might be in danger at a time when it was impossible for him to help her.

He had met her when the work of Washington's Secret Service and that of the Department had merged, and they had made a bargain not to give up their work while the war lasted.

The sound of Oundle precariously balancing a tray on one

hand, while at the same time kicking the door to with his foot, woke Loftus with a start.

Grumbling good temperedly, he sat up, while Oundle found a place for the tray, and began to pour out. "Thanks, Ned. Anything through?"

"Thornton kept on the lovely's heels. She went back to the Cherry."

"Yes?" Loftus sipped the hot tea, gratefully.

"She inquired a great deal about the Errols," went on Oundle. "Her story was that she had been told by a friend to give them a message, or something to that effect, and she'd forgotten their address. Someone at the club supplied it."

"Did she go there?"

"No. It was an errand of inquiry. Were they in the Army or this and that? Most surprised to find that they weren't, but perhaps they were the wrong people—her friend had been rather vague about it. In short she gave herself a cover, and then nipped back to her flat, 34 Byng Court."

"Hm-hmm. The address Mark gave me last night. Anything else?"

"A moan from Carruthers," said Oundle with a smile. "He had the lady's visitor to follow, and lost him in the black-out, so he went back to the flat. About an hour afterwards the man returned, and, I'm sorry to say, didn't come out again."

"Did he get back before the girl?"

"Yes, by an hour."

"What then?"

"I sent reinforcements, and Spats Thornton and Carry came off duty. This woman must be a beauty, Bill, even Spats went off the deep end about her."

"Damn the woman. What's the man like?"

"They didn't get much of a look, but agreed on his toughness. Evening dress and all that, but a pretty noticeable hairy heel."

"Whose name is the flat in?"

"Hers. Myra Berne."

"The man's our meat," said Loftus. "Pour me out another cup, will you?" He lit a cigarette, and closed his eyes for a moment. "Yes, the man's our problem. I fancy the woman will be used to decoy us from our straight and narrow path."

Oundle scowled. "That's sheer guesswork."

"Not entirely," asserted Loftus. "She was a decoy for Arkeld all right. Everyone tries the same old tricks, my son, time has shown that they work. Mike's the most likely to succumb, isn't he?"

Oundle scratched his chin.

"Dammit, there's no reason to think that she . . ."

"There's every reason in the world," said Loftus firmly. "She asks about Mike and Mark, so she's on to them. She'll probably angle for a meeting, and apologise for this mistake about her friend and see what develops. Ring Mike to come over—no," he amended, "I'll go and see him, there's the little merchant to attend to."

Loftus finished his tea, slipped out of bed, bathed and dressed in quick time, and was ready when a waiter brought breakfast from the restaurant.

It was a meal he particularly enjoyed, but he did not linger over it that morning. In less than half an hour he was walking briskly towards the Errols' flat. There was no one in the street except tradesmen whom he recognised as regulars, and there was no sign that the Errols' flat was being watched. He made a mental note to find what flats opposite and nearby were empty—or had recently been let—and then knocked at the flat door.

Wally Davidson opened it.

Wally looked tired; he rarely looked anything else. Loftus knew him well enough to be sure that he had had a good night's sleep, and that there had been no trouble. The Errols greeted him somewhat exuberantly, although Mark was on the quiet side. They had taken turns in watching their prisoner, who had slept most of the night on his couch.

Loftus went into the room where he was lying.

He removed the gag and ear-plugs, while Davidson gave the man a glass of water. He drank eagerly.

"What the 'ell d'yer think yer doing?"

Despite the truculence of his words there was fear in him. Brought to a state of hunger, thirst, cramp and weariness, he was obviously not in a position to hold out much longer.

Loftus said:

"I'm going to find out who you are, where you come from, and who you work for. If you refuse, I've special authority to deal with you the way I think best. Got that?"

The man's eyes wavered.

"In case it hasn't sunk in," said Loftus, "I'll give you five minutes to think about it."

He turned away abruptly. Davidson followed him, and the door was closed. Mark Errol said quickly:

"Will he talk?"

"Looks remarkably like it," said Loftus confidently. "I'll give him a few minutes to make sure."

Afterwards, he knew that it was a mistake, but there was nothing to indicate that at the moment. Had he started questioning the man right away he might have had some obstinacy to overcome, and he had no desire to use force if it could be avoided. The five minutes would produce a mental condition, he believed, which would make the man more amenable.

But hardly had he reached the other room than the telephone rang, and Mike Errol answered it. He held out the receiver.

"It's Gordon."

"Right, thanks," said Loftus, and took the receiver. The call might be one of mere routine, or it might be fraught with many complications; he judged from Craigie's crisp and serious voice that it was more likely the latter.

"Get over at once, will you," Craigie said. "And bring Ned."

"Right. I'll be there in fifteen minutes." Loftus replaced the receiver, and then dialled Ned Oundle's number. The Errols and Davidson were watching the big man closely, all of them aware that there might be developments of first-class importance.

"Gordon sounded as if we're for it," said Loftus with a faint smile. "But there's work for you, my friends. Mike, the lovely you seem to be so enthusiastic about is looking for you." He gave no time for that to sink in or heed to Mike's exclamation, following on with swift instructions to be where the woman might easily find him—at Cherry's or similar haunts. Mike did not look displeased.

"What about me?" demanded Mark aggressively.

"You're after the boy-friend of Byng Court, you and Wally together," said Loftus. "Find out all you can about the gentleman—Miller at the Yard may be able to help a bit—and get it fast."

"What about the Shrimp?" Wally demanded.

"Ring the Yard, and have him collected for the time being," said Loftus. "We can get him out of Cannon Row later, if needs be. Ask the Yard about the girl, too—child, if you prefer it—they might know of her. All set?"

Oundle's arrival coincided with their nods of satisfaction. The two men hurried downstairs and into Oundle's car.

Loftus looked swiftly up and down the street. "It looks as if they've given their little man up as hopeless, but we can't be too sure. I'll get up to the office right away, and you phone from a call-box to the Yard. Ask Miller to make inquiries about flats opposite or near ours—and it might be an idea if his men had a look through any empty ones for signs of recent habitation. Got that?"

"Why don't I ring from Gordon's office?" objected Oundle.

"Because it will lose another four or five minutes, and I've lost plenty already," said Loftus.

Oundle pulled up near the side-turning from which the office was reached. They had not been followed, although that was not necessarily good news—Loftus would have liked to feel that someone was on his heels. He was more worried by the apparent inaction of the other side than he would have been by any demonstration of hostility.

He put that thought aside when he reached Craigie's office.

Craigie was alone, his expression one of deep anxiety. An expression so alien to the Department leader's usual composure and calm caused Loftus to move forward quickly.

"What's gone wrong, Gordon?"

Craigie said: "Arkeld was murdered last night." He pushed a hand over his thinning hair, and added quietly:

"A cargo ship with a full load of Argentine beef was blown up last night. It was ready for unloading this morning. Seven soldiers guarding it were killed, half-a-dozen others were injured. It was at Liverpool, and intended for the seventh area."

Loftus said evenly:

"The seventh, eh? So it's spreading?"

"It looks like it. Of course, it might have been intended for any area as far as the crew and others knew—but . . ."

"I know," said Loftus. "They bring it across the Atlantic, they get it through hell and worse, and when it's safely in dock it blows up and there's nothing to show for all that heroism and fortitude. No question that it was sabotage, I suppose?"

"None at all—there were no raids up there last night."

"And Arkeld was murdered about the same time. Where was he?"

"In London," said Craigie with a gesture of resignation. "I had to take all of you off, you know that. The regional directors and Mortimer were at the Landon Hotel for a conference, and Arkeld was to make a statement. They were all staying in the same hotel. So I got the police to watch, it was certain, I thought, that there would be no funny business while they were together like that. Howover—someone got in and shot him."

"No chance of suicide?"

"Not the slightest. There was no gun."

"Oh, well," said Loftus. "I suppose I'd better go over, although there isn't likely to be much to find. The police are on to it, I suppose?"

"Miller's there himself."

"That's something," said Loftus. As he spoke, the green light showed again, and Oundle was admitted. Craigie nodded a greeting, then turned back to Loftus:

"It alters a great deal, Bill. We can't safely leave any of the regional directors or Mortimer unattended, and they don't know what's happening yet! I've had the P.M. on the phone, and he has an idea that they should all be told, so that they can look for leakages in the areas under their control. What do you think of it?"

"I don't," said Loftus briskly. "Will Hershall insist?"

"I think he'll leave it to us."

"Tell him that if we've got to look for leakages I think we ought to start from the top, will you?" said Loftus. "And tell him also that if the trouble is starting from outside, we're more likely to get results if the directors don't realise that there is danger on a major scale."

"You mean that they'll be more easily approached by our unknown enemy, and we will have more chance of seeing who does the approaching," said Craigie with a slow smile. "I think he'll be happy enough to let us go our own way for a few days, but only if we get results."

Loftus grinned. "He's a man for results, bless him! But there's no reason why they—the directors—shouldn't know that we're investigating Arkeld's murder and the thirty-ninth area trouble." He looked thoughtful for a moment, and Craigie said quietly:

"You'd like to look in at the conference, is that it?"

"Can you fix it?"

"I'll try," said Craigie.

He felt better when Loftus and Oundle had left, for Loftus gave him a feeling of assurance which at times was apt to grow thin. Craigie had the same effect on the big man; neither knew of their mutual sources of inspiration. But Craigie was smiling a little as he telephoned Number 10, spoke first to Smythe, the P.M.'s confidential secretary, and then to the Prime Minister himself. Hershall raised no objections to Loftus's suggestion.

"He can have three days," he said decisively. "All right, Craigie, thanks for ringing."

Loftus, meanwhile, was on the way to the Landon Hotel. All was quiet. It seemed that the newspapers had not yet heard of the murder. He asked for the manager, and soon afterwards was ushered, with Oundle, into a suite on the second floor. On the way—the manager accompanied them—Loftus learned that the six gentlemen on whom depended the regional distribution of the nation's food had occupied suites on the same floor.

"Who suggested that?" Loftus had asked.

"It was my idea, sir. And Sir Bruce Mortimer was good enough to commend it. It made it easy for them to get assembled for informal discussion at almost any time."

The door of Suite 18 was opened by a plain-clothes policeman standing outside. The first room was empty. The second contained four men, one of them dead.

Arkeld had been shot in bed.

The bullet had entered his right temple, and the result was not pleasant. Two men were arranging a camera tripod, one of them a finger-print expert. The third man was Superintendent Miller, Special Branch Chief at Scotland Yard.

His face, a large one and rugged, with broad features and a look of good-humour—was distinguished by a pair of shrewd light blue eyes. He nodded to Loftus and Oundle, whom he knew well.

The camera-work was soon finished, and the sheet replaced.

"Well, what do you make of it?" Loftus asked Miller.

"What do you?" asked Miller. "You can see what I can see."

Loftus turned back the sheet again, noting the sharp and somewhat severe features of the murdered man. His eye travelled from the bullet wound to the window, and then to the door.

"Well, he certainly wasn't shot through the window or the door if he was lying on the bed. And if he was shot from closer by, there would have been more damage. A biggish bullet, wasn't it?"

"A .45," said Miller. "You've got it in one, Loftus. He wasn't lying on the bed when he was shot, but the pillow and the sheets were drenched in blood, so he might have been carried here immediately afterwards. The only time anything was heard which could have been the shot was at twelve o'clock last night—and," said Miller quietly, "at twelve o'clock, if I'm to believe what I'm told, he was with the Director-General and the regional directors."

Loftus said: "Why should they lie? When was this discovered?"

"About an hour and a half ago."

"What does the surgeon say?"

"He can't give the time of death much nearer than 'within three hours of midnight'," said Miller. "It doesn't help us a lot. But . . ." his face showed a glimmer of a smile—"it's your job, Loftus. Or so I'm told."

"We're co-operating," said Loftus promptly. "You heard what might have been a shot about midnight. And . . ."

He stopped, then. He had to, for from somewhere inside the hotel, and not far away, there came the roar of an explosion so violent that the whole building seemed to rock. They stared at each other, tense and alarmed, before Miller said hoarsely:

"The conference is meeting now, *in the hotel.* And that came from downstairs."

7

CONFERENCE IN CONFUSION

L oftus reached the door before Miller, and seeing this, Miller held back. He knew his limitations, and he knew the qualities of Loftus. He believed that the large man would be more effective with Mortimer and the others, and that the presence of a policeman, even one of high rank, might hamper him.

Pictures which had been hanging in the passage were either on the floor or askew, and the thick red carpet was covered with fallen plaster. Cracks showed, but Miller did not think that they were deep. He was wondering what course to take when Sergeant Adams, an elephantine man much shrewder than his appearance suggested, appeared at the end of the corridor. Adams was dishevelled and had a slight cut in one cheek.

Miller said sharply:

"Where was the explosion? The conference room?"

"No, sir. In a cupboard fairly near to it. Mr. Loftus has just gone into the conference room."

Miller rubbed his chin.

"Right. Then we'll wait until he sends us a message, Adams."

In the conference room six gentlemen, two secretaries and William Loftus, were foregathered.

When Loftus had entered it was plain that there had been some alarm, and the state of the room indicated that the ceiling had suffered fairly severely. One heavy portrait—of the dozen that lined the walls—was on the floor, and several small panes of glass in the windows were broken. Three chairs and a writing-bureau were lying on their sides.

It was not difficult for Loftus to imagine that before the explosion the directors had been sitting round the long, horseshoe shaped table, going through items on an agenda which remained on the table in front of Sir Bruce Mortimer's chair. There would have been the minimum of formality; their getting together at the Landon Hotel suggesting an intention of doing things rather more quickly than was usually their custom.

Loftus knew Sir Bruce reasonably well.

He had been watching that gentleman for three days, although Mortimer did not know it, and in the course of the three days Mortimer had contrived to get through an amount of work which was gargantuan in its proportions. He was an odd combination. Though untiringly industrious, traditional ways of procedure mattered to him, and he was guided by them. No one could deny his ability, his shrewdness, his genuine desire to do his best, his knowledge of his subject; if only he would have prised himself from his love of red tape he would have had few critics. But it seemed that he had been a civil servant too long. Loftus believed that the Minister of Food would have transferred his Director-General of Distribution if he had been able to find any other capable of the divers duties.

It was Mortimer who spoke when Loftus entered.

"There is nothing we want, thank you."

Loftus walked right in and closed the door.

"I told you . . ." began Mortimer, and then he stopped and looked a little startled. He was standing by his seat, a tall, white-haired aristocratic-looking man, with thin, aquiline features, and very light blue eyes. He looked piercingly at Loftus. "I have already told the manager we are *quite* untouched."

"Sorry," said Loftus. "The report didn't reach me. I was upstairs with the police, gentlemen, and—well," he added with a shrug of his shoulders, "I was naturally a little afraid that something had happened here. Are you continuing with the business of the day?"

"Certainly we are," said Mortimer. "What is your name, please?"

"Loftus."

It would not be true to say that Mortimer thawed, or that his manner grew any more human, but there was a definite change in him. "You have been sent from—er . . ."

"The Department," said Loftus gently.

"Ah. We were discussing you before the explosion. It will perhaps be best if you meet the directors." He presented Loftus to each man separately with a formality which gave the Department agent an opportunity to weigh up and assess: he needed that opportunity.

Lord Brelling was first.

A short, thickset man with wiry red hair, Brelling gave the impression of being an aggressive self-made man. That was true. He had started life as a grocer's errand boy, and within twenty years had become the owner of the largest chain of grocery shops in the country. His stores were popular and well-run; it was said that he had a genius for choosing the right men to act for him. Certainly no better choice could have been made for the task of controlling one of the regional areas of food distribution and conservation. He nodded amiably enough to Loftus.

Sir Augustus Gray, a thin whippet of man, had similar qualifications. One would never be surprised to see him standing behind a counter. There was the faintest suggestion of foxiness in his thin features, and small brown eyes, yet he had an irreproachable reputation, and he was one of the few men who, after making progress in the world of commerce, had gone to Oxford and graduated—at one time he had been the oldest undergraduate at the University. A man, it was said, who did everything thoroughly, and one who did not easily forgive mistakes.

He smiled briefly without speaking.

Sir John Sanderson was a different type of man. Mellow and middle-aged, his fortune and business had been inherited, his interest in it developing only after the war had started. No one quite knew why he had been chosen as the midland regional director. Loftus, who saw the reports of most things that went through Craigie's office, knew that Sanderson's area ran neck and neck with Brelling's; both were well-equipped and well-organised. A grey-haired man with a pale face, Sanderson was well-known to most newspaper readers, for his interest in cricket and racing made him one of the most influential men in sport.

"I hope we don't keep you too busy," he said, his expression one of kindly interest.

Next to Sanderson was Mr. Daniel Fortescue, managing-director of a multiple-store business which operated exclusively in the north and north midlands. Broad and burly, he both looked, and spoke, as a north countryman.

"Ah'm pleased to know you, Loftus."

And then Loftus looked at the fifth regional director, trying to clear his mind of prejudice. He had always disliked Mr. Edward Whittaker, who not only ran a chainstore business, but owned one of the lesser national dailies, and a string of provincial papers which faithfully echoed his views. Before the war he had been an isolationist, adamantly opposed to all foreign commitments. He had said bitter things about the agreements which, he claimed, had precipitated the war. He had taken little part in public life until the fall of the first war Government, when a seat had been found for him in the House, and he had been appointed regional director of food for Scotland. That had caused a flurry, for the Scots had wanted a Scotsman. But for all his unpopularity he was an efficient and thorough man. Loftus believed that Hershall had chosen him as he did everyone—on qualifications alone.

Whittaker gave Loftus a cold nod, and turned aside abruptly; in profile his likeness to a fish was undoubtedly increased, his eyes being frosty yet filmed, his forehead and chin negligible.

"And now," said Mortimer, "perhaps we can arrange some order out of the confusion into which the conference has been thrown. We were requested to allow you to be present, Mr. Loftus, although I am not sure in what way you expect to be of assistance."

Loftus said: "I'd like to make sure that no one is in danger, Sir Bruce."

There was a faint, even supercilious lift of Mortimer's right eyebrow.

"What kind of danger do you imply?"

"I'm not sure what form it might take," said Loftus. "Have you drawn any conclusions from the events of the past twelve hours?"

Mortimer tightened his lips, and Sanderson said comfortably:

"You mean from poor Arkeld's death and the explosion, Mr. Loftus?"

"That's right."

"It's obvious, isn't it?" said Whittaker sharply. "The explosion occurred in an ante-room next to the smaller conference room, where we might have been expected to meet. It was deliberately aimed at injuring us."

"Oh, nonsense," said Sanderson. "I don't believe that for a moment."

"No?" asked Whittaker, and he made the word into a sneer.

Loftus began to enjoy himself. Now that he saw that none of them had been hurt he was able to approach the matter in a completely detached frame of mind, and he was interested to see that there were differences between at least two of the directors. It was not hard to understand that Whittaker and Sanderson would not get along well.

"We were discussing it before you arrived," said Mortimer, and he gave the impression that he considered the discussion quite out of place. "Have you any definite opinion?"

"It's too early for that," said Loftus.

"Naturally, naturally," said Gray, who had a habit of repeating single words and treating them as a complete sentence. "Nevertheless, I agree with Whittaker."

"Fiddlesticks," said Brelling clearly.

"It's downreet nonsense," added Fortescue gruffly.

"It looks to me," said Loftus with a smile, "as if we're going to get no further discussing it without the full facts, gentlemen. But may I suggest we go on with the original purpose of the meeting?"

The only man who answered was Fortescue.

"Aye, that's reet. Let's get down to brass tacks."

Loftus reflected that the nerves of all of them were steady enough, and that they could be commended for not being put into any kind of a panic because of an explosion which might well have been directed against them. He listened as the meeting droned on, with his eyes half-closed.

It was interesting, but no more.

The conference that morning had been called to discuss the difficulties which Arkeld was experiencing, and it appeared that Mortimer had sent out to all the regional directors a questionnaire about similar troubles. The directors had collated their information and were here to report.

The reports gave nothing away.

Until the ship which had been blown up that morning, or the previous night, there had been no trouble which could be construed as sabotage. There had been accidents and damage caused by bombing, the latter negligible since the main stores were kept underground. Nothing which suggested organised sabotage had been forthcoming; Arkeld's area alone had suffered from that.

Loftus was thinking.

"They've sized up the possibility of sabotage all right, and I might just as well have agreed with Hershall without arguing. They know as much as I do."

He reflected that he had been wrong to think that Mortimer would miss the inference for the trouble in the thirty-ninth area. Mortimer missed nothing, and Mortimer was already on the point of suggesting to the regional directors that they searched their departments for possible sources of leakage. Loftus, without quite knowing why he felt so strongly, did not want that to happen, and he judged the right moment for saying:

"May I have a word, Sir Bruce?"

Mortimer inclined his head.

"It isn't a great deal," Loftus went on, "but I have been looking into the trouble with the thirty-ninth area, and one thing appears quite certain—it is all outside work."

Mortimer frowned.

"Are you sure of that?"

"As far as I can be, yes," said Loftus. "There hasn't been a lot of time yet, of course, but I—and when I say 'I' please understand that I mean my Department—think that the sabotage has been very well organised amongst the work-people."

Mortimer leaned back in his chair.

"Indeed?"

"I'm not going to try to put details forward," said Loftus, "but I don't need to tell any of you of the insidious work of reactionaries even today. The thirty-ninth area, being in the midland district, is one which covers a wide section of the population—a section which can perhaps be more easily approached by propagandists than any other. In short, I think that there is a network of reactionaries who seek an opportunity for creating damage, and seize it when it is presented."

"That is not my conclusion," said Mortimer sharply.

"I'm sorry," said Loftus quietly, "but the evidence supports it."

He looked at Mortimer squarely, and he saw the man's eyes narrow. Mortimer made no further comment, however, and Fortescue broke in.

"The bloody Communists again, I suppose?"

"It's too early to say that," said Loftus.

"Damn it, man, don't beat about the bush," said Fortescue. "You won't help the thing by hedging it about wi' words." He spoke bluntly, and yet without irritation. "It's the Reds ye've got in mind, isn't it?"

Loftus shrugged.

"Since you must have it, yes."

"They might be anywhere," said Whittaker.

"But there is a central organisation," said Loftus quickly, "and I want to find it. I think myself—I submit this as an opinion, gentlemen—that it would be wise if we gave no one the impression that we are alarmed. I think Sir Thomas Arkeld's death might well be made public as natural or accidental. It is not the time to cause any alarm about food."

"Too true it's not," said Fortescue. "The people have been wonderful one way and the other, and ah'll deal wi' any man who says differently. But if they think their food's in danger— Ah wouldn't like to say what they'll do."

Brelling cleared his throat.

"That's exactly it, Fortescue." He turned to Loftus. "How quickly do you think you can get results?"

"I hope it won't be more than a week."

"A week?" Mortimer was coldly surprised. "It is a matter which appears to warrant much longer attention than that."

"The final clear-up will take longer, of course," said Loftus, and he spoke as if he were quite certain that he knew how to tackle the problem, "but *if* I'm right—and I think I am, gentlemen—then a week will see the end of the leaders of the organisation. You won't expect me to say more now?"

"And if we do expect it, you won't," said Whittaker sneeringly.

"Right," said Loftus.

Brelling chuckled.

"You don't mince words, do you? What do you think about it, Mortimer?"

"Since we have not been able to get Arkeld's report," said Mortimer, "we can obviously only leave the matter in Mr. Loftus's hands for the time being. He is fully aware of the importance of it, and the need for losing no time—*and* the danger of working too quickly and therefore carelessly." A barb, thought Loftus with an inward smile.

"Isn't there a copy of Arkeld's report?" asked Gray.

"There is not." Mortimer's voice was crisp. "All the papers which he brought with him were stolen, and I believe they contained a full plan of the arrangements in his area. I have already instructed his deputy to make alterations as quickly as possible. And now . . ." he looked at Loftus—"we have to discuss Arkeld's successor, and make a recommendation. Do you need to stay for that, Mr. Loftus?"

"Thank you, no," said Loftus.

He nodded all round; the only man who did not acknowledge it was Whittaker. Loftus wondered briefly whether he was allowing personal dislike to crystallise into unjustified suspicion, then dismissed Whittaker from his mind. It was disturbing news that Arkeld's papers had been stolen. It opened up possibilities which had not yet been considered, and he was not anxious for additional complications. He returned to the room Arkeld had occupied, nodding to the man on duty at the door.

As he did so he heard a slight scuffling sound.

Yet the room was empty. It surprised him, for he had expected to find Miller there, or one of the other policemen. He stepped through into the bedroom to find that the body had been removed, as well as the bedding; no one was there.

The bathroom and a small dressing-room, which made up the suite, were also empty, and yet he was sure that he had heard the sound.

The dressing-room had another door leading to the passage. Loftus passed through this, and approached the guard.

"No one came out while I was going in, did they?"

"I saw no one, sir."

"Hmm. Keep your eyes open. And where is the Superintendent?"

"He asked you to telephone him at the office, sir."

"Right, thanks. I . . ."

Loftus stopped in the middle of a sentence, for he saw the door opening behind the guard. It opened from the inside, although he had been through the rooms and made sure they were empty. As he moved forward a figure slipped out and began to run at startling speed towards the stairs and the lift— a figure so small that it could have been hidden almost anywhere, a male figure remarkably like that of Topsy's in stature.

It ran without a sound.

8

"QUITE A CIRCUS"

L oftus ran also, but not silently. He pounded along the passage, his bulk hiding the small figure from the guard.

The man, or boy—or for that matter Topsy dressed in male clothes—showed a turn of speed which was almost fantastic. With a flying leap he was astride the wide handrail, sliding downwards with such speed that Loftus had only a vague blur in his mind as he started down the stairs, jumping the last half-dozen, steadying himself and then starting for the next.

Without an instant of hesitation the tiny figure turned the curve in the handrail like a stunt cyclist on the Wall of Death. The staircase did not end in the foyer, but in a wide passage leading from it. The passage was empty.

The creature turned towards the foyer, and reached it eight yards ahead of Loftus. When the latter came in sight of the crowd of people standing there, he saw his quarry dart straight towards the doors. Nothing impeded him.

Loftus was not so lucky.

It was the broad back of a middle-aged woman which

stopped him. He tried to dodge her, but she had slipped against a chair, almost falling into his path.

He staggered to one side.

The collision had rocketed the woman forward, and she would have fallen but for the presence of mind of a tall, fair-haired man standing close by.

"What on earth are you up to?" demanded Carruthers disapprovingly. Loftus looked up and recognised his fellow agent.

Breathing heavily he gasped: "Did you—see—it?"

"See it? See what?"

"Blast—you. Small—creature. Ask . . ."

He pointed weakly towards the door, and then subsided into a chair. His breath back, he apologised profusely to the lady with whom he had collided, then moved cautiously towards a returning Carruthers.

"Any luck?"

"Not much," said Carruthers glumly. "The commissionaire saw him—her—or it—dodging away. A dwarf, he thought. Any truth in it?"

"I'd say so," said Loftus ruefully. "And composed entirely of india-rubber if his movements are any criterion." He walked a little stiffly towards the stairs. "We'll have another look round Arkeld's room before we go any further. What brought you along, old man?"

Carruthers smiled.

"I woke up early and phoned Craigie. He said I might find you here."

"Any message?"

"No."

"Well, that's something," said Loftus.

There was nothing in Arkeld's room to suggest that there had been an illegal visitor, but to Loftus it seemed obvious that the dwarf would not have been there without a purpose—and the purpose obviously was to get something which had not been secured with the papers taken when Arkeld had been murdered.

There were other problems branching from that.

Mortimer had told him that Arkeld had been robbed, but Miller had not mentioned it. True, Miller had had little time before the explosion had taken their attention from the immediate problem. Loftus stepped to the telephone of the room, and called the Yard.

Miller was soon on the other line.

"Yes," he said to Loftus's question. "The clothes and suitcases were there, but the portfolio which Arkeld always carried with his papers was missing."

"Who told you he always carried it?"

"His secretary."

"Where is he?"

"It isn't a he," said Miller, "it's a she, and she told me over the telephone that he always carried his papers in a black calf portfolio. He had it with him when he left Bedford yesterday."

"Your men checked him," said Loftus. "Anything to report?"

"Nothing at all—it was a straightforward journey, and he wasn't followed."

"Hmm," said Loftus. "Did you tell Mortimer that the portfolio was missing?"

"Yes."

"And the others?"

"No. He asked me to let him tell the rest, and I wasn't sorry about that. What's on your mind, Loftus?"

"I don't quite know," said Loftus. "I can't measure it up, old man. Arkeld was presumably killed in the hotel, but not necessarily on the bed . . ."

"Almost certainly not on the bed," said Miller. "I've checked the details. A bullet from a .45 would have made far more mess if it had been fired from close quarters, and in the position he was lying he could only be shot at close quarters."

"Ye-es. I agree with you. He was killed somewhere else, but presumably taken to the bed to bleed to death there."

"Why 'presumably'?" asked Miller.

"Because it isn't an established fact," said Loftus. "Will you get one of your brighter police-surgeons to examine the pillow and find whether the blood on it checks with that of Arkeld's? I'm wondering," he added slowly, "if the blood on the pillow could have been put there to make us think he was killed in his room—it's a possibility."

"Ye-es. I'll see to that," said Miller, and he paused for a moment. "You know what you're implying, don't you?"

Loftus smiled into the telephone.

"I do, Superintendent!"

"Is there anything else?"

"The servant who heard the shot, or thought he did. What's his name?"

"Farrow. He's a night-waiter, and he was taking tea to someone on the same floor."

"Good," said Loftus. "Ring me at the flat or the office when the surgeon's through, will you?" He replaced the receiver, and then called the hotel exchange, and asked for the waiter named Farrow to be sent up to him. He was asked to hold on, and then he was told that Farrow had gone off duty.

"Will you find me his address and let me have it," said Loftus sharply.

When he replaced the receiver again, Carruthers was standing by the window.

"Am I to know anything about it?"

"Later," said Loftus briefly. "At the moment just listen, resisting firmly the burbling up of bright ideas.

"Arkeld was killed either (a) in the hotel or (b) outside," said Loftus, thinking aloud, "and (b) isn't very likely. He was in pyjamas, and with a man killed in that fashion it would be virtually impossible to dress him in anything without getting blood about. But you can have too much blood, and a wound in the head shouldn't bleed as much as that one did. Apart from the dressing difficulty it is asking too much to say that he could have been carried, quite dead, into the hotel and to his room." Loftus paused.

"So he was killed inside," said Carruthers.

"All right," said Loftus. "He was killed inside, and in his own suite or one of the others. Presumably he was carried to his bed—certainly he wasn't shot there. Other suites on the same floor could have been the scene of it, then—he could have been carried easily from one to the other. And . . ." he paused again, and Carruthers widened his eyes.

"By George, one of the directors . . ."

"It could be," said Loftus. "We'll find who else has a suite or a room on this floor. The waiter was carrying tea to someone about midnight. It could have been one of the crowd, of course, or it could have been someone quite independent. One way and another I wish it were that."

Carruthers grimaced. "Rather than treachery in high places?"

"There isn't time or room for delicate handling," said Loftus. "It's a possibility and remains one until we've disproved it. This business is growing, Carry. I wonder if the others have had any luck?"

Carruthers had no time to ask what the others were doing, for the telephone rang again. It was the manager. He gave Loftus Farrow's address, pointing out that the police had given the man permission to go. He also mentioned that three people independent of the regional directors had suites on the first floor, adding earnestly:

"You will be discreet, Mr. Loftus, won't you? I don't wish to cause any inconvenience and I know your task is extremely difficult, but—well, our guests are not easily appeased sometimes, and things have been so difficult that we don't want to incur their displeasure."

"I won't cause bother unless it's necessary, certainly. Who are the other people?"

"One is a lady who—but perhaps I had better come and see you, Mr. Loftus."

"I think perhaps you had," said Loftus, and he hung up. He hesitated for a moment, and then rubbed his chin. "Carry, get back to the Errols' flat. I told Ned to wait there until police took charge inside and out, but I'm a bit uneasy about it. Ring me as soon as you're there, will you?"

"Right," said Carruthers promptly.

Loftus waited alone for several minutes, and judging from his expression his mind was quite blank. It was. He did not want to confuse himself with too many diversions, and he needed a mind as open as it could be. Consequently he stared out of the window, and hummed a little ditty which was at least six years out of date. Thus the manager found him.

The manager was a Frenchman named Leroux, but only by an occasional gesture did he betray his nationality. He was of medium height, slim, discreetly dressed, his manner perfectly attuned to the wealthy guests who from time to time stayed at the Landon.

Loftus looked woodenly into the suave face and watchful dark eyes.

"I know that my request seems a little strange in the circumstances," said Leroux quietly, "and it might, possibly, have annoyed you, Mr. Loftus, but . . ." he shrugged—"the tragedy is already affecting some of the guests, and it is a long time since we have been busy. We were just picking up. However, I will not waste time with my own troubles. The guests on this floor, apart from those whom you already know, are all foreigners. The one to whom Farrow was taking tea last night is an American. He is a semi-invalid, and his named is Rannigan."

Loftus nodded.

"The second is a Greek named Letaxa," said Leroux, "a business man who is negotiating for a Greek loan. I have that information in confidence, Mr. Loftus, but it is fair that you should know. The public, of course, do not know the real reason for his visit."

Again Loftus nodded.

"The third . . ." Leroux gave an expressive shrug of the shoulders—"is *La Reine*. Need I say more?"

Loftus did not speak immediately, but Leroux saw the hardening of his eyes, and noticed the slight tightening of the muscles of his face.

"*La Reine*, you say. How long has she been here?"

"Five days."

"How long does she propose to stay?"

"She told me that if she received the attention that she considered necessary she would stay through the summer, Mr. Loftus."

"Oh," said Loftus. "All right, and thanks very much I won't disturb any of them if it can be avoided."

Leroux bowed suavely and withdrew.

Left to himself, Loftus reflected on the presence of the lady who styled herself *La Reine*. He did not know her personally, but he knew her reputation. She was one of the most famous musical comedy stars of pre-war Paris. She had been in London during the fall of France, stayed there until the bombing started, and then gone to the country. Despite the immensity of the war news, there had alway been space in the Press for information about *La Reine's* movements.

It was hard to say why.

There have been other musical comedy actresses as famous, and yet she had the "something" which made her news wherever she went and whatever the circumstances. She was beautiful, but it was not her beauty or her dancing or her voice, which gave *La Reine* that little something which no one else had got. It was her superb horsemanship. An odd thing in musical comedy, but she had first taken London and then Paris by storm with her performance on a white horse. A perfect animal, trained to absolute precision.

It was fairly well known that *La Reine* had graduated to the stage from the sawdust ring. She had been an equestrienne in the circus of a man whom Loftus could not remember, before reaching her present eminence.

Damn it, what *was* the man's name?

Walking along the passage Loftus saw that the police guard was still on duty, and that the servants were busily clearing up the mess after the explosion. It occurred to Loftus that he had been far more concerned with the effect of the bang than with the origin of it, and he hoped that Miller was making good this omission.

Outside the Landon he took a taxi, aware of an unexplainable need for urgency. He thought of the prisoner and his strangely deep voice, and told the cabby to hurry. As the cab turned into Brook Street, his lips tightened and his heart missed a beat, for there was no mistaking the shape of an ambulance that was standing outside the Errols' flat, nor the several policemen about the doorway.

The cab drew up, and Loftus leapt to the ground. A policeman recognised him and stood aside. But Loftus did not go far, for when he reached the foot of the stairs he met two attendants carrying a stretcher.

He saw the face of Wally Davidson, and knew that he was badly hurt.

There was no sign of Carruthers.

9

OF MAXIMILIAN GOLT

Heavy-hearted, Loftus walked up the stairs.

The door of the flat was open, and he saw a police-sergeant and, further in the room, Carruthers. So Carry was all right, and that was something to be thankful for. Both men were staring at the floor, or what appeared to be the floor.

Actually it was the body of their late prisoner.

He had been strangled, and his mottled face did not make a pleasant sight.

Carruthers half-turned, hard-faced.

"How's Wally?" asked Loftus. "Has a doctor seen him?"

"Yes, I sent for one as soon as I arrived," said Carruthers. "He was shot. Operation at once. Touch and go."

Loftus nodded. "What did you find?"

"Wally there." Carruthers pointed to one side of the room on which there was a dark patch of blood. "And this fellow just as he is now. Except that Wally's gone, nothing has been touched. Did you expect this?"

"I saw it as a possibility," Loftus said seriously. "That's why I sent Ned along. He and Wally together might have outmatched them. This is no affair for one man on his own. Where *is* Ned? He should have been here half-an-hour before you."

"There isn't a sign of him."

Loftus turned authoritatively: "Sergeant! I want to find out if a Mr. Oundle has been seen within the past hour. It's urgent."

"Of course, sir. Actually . . ." it was a youngish man, and clearly he did not know how much respect to show to Loftus; he was inclined to be on the generous side with it. "Actually I was here on duty—I had instructions to search through empty flats, and I was doing that when I was sent for by a man on the beat. There is a flat opposite which is empty, but several cigarette ends were found in the front room."

Loftus said furiously: "What a ruddy fool I am—if I'd played my hunch right out this wouldn't have happened. Have you those cigarette ends with you?"

"Yes, sir." The sergeant took them from an envelope, and Loftus selected two.

"You'll want the other for your report," he said. He knew that people were smoking brands which in peacetime they would not have looked at, but he also knew that Alexis cigarettes, such as these, were an exclusive brand, made by hand in a small shop off Piccadilly.

"You've recognised them?" he asked.

"Yes, sir."

"Get me a list of their customers if you can," said Loftus briskly. "And I've an idea—only an idea and it might be a wash-out, but we'll see. I'm leaving the photographing and all the rest to you, but I don't think you'll get much help from finger-prints."

Loftus hurried downstairs with Carruthers on his heels. Once in the street he began to search the kerb and pavement with slow, painstaking method. A policeman walked towards them and Loftus looked up sharply.

"How often are the streets cleaned at nights, these days?"

"It depends what kind of a night it's been, sir."

"Was this done last night?"

"Let me see—no, it wasn't, the pavement's usually wet from the water-cart when I come on duty, and it was as dry as a bone when I arrived this morning."

"Good," said Loftus. "Thanks."

"Can I ask what we're looking for?" asked Carruthers.

"Cigarette ends, old boy, particularly of the brand Alexis—and, by George, there is one!"

The end which he picked up was actually a cigarette little more than half-smoked. There were three others along the kerb, all of them long enough for the gold lettering of the brand to be easily visible. Loftus put them in an envelope, and straightened up.

"What does it prove?" asked Carruthers drily.

"That the man in the room of the empty flat smoked the same cigarettes as the man in the grey bowler who fired at the Errols yesterday," said Loftus. He added abruptly: "Do you remember the circus story of *La Reine?*"

"Who doesn't?"

"Do you remember her manager—the circus owner who made her!"

Carruthers frowned in concentration, and then shook his head. Loftus shrugged, while from the other side of the road there came a gruff voice demanding to know whether he was to wait or whether he had been forgotten. It was Loftus's cabby. Loftus stepped towards him.

"Fleet Street," he said. "We'll try the *Daily Express* office. In a hurry, please."

The driver obeyed that instruction, and was told to wait

again while they went inside the glass-walled building of the
Daily Express. A clerk on duty turned out the ten year old files
of the story of *La Reine* in less than ten minutes.

Loftus read swiftly.

"That's him—Golt, Maximilian Golt. And there is the
gentleman." He looked at the heavy, reproduced features of
Maximilian Golt. "I'm a thorough nuisance, I know, but do
you think there might be a profile photograph of this man?"

"I'll see, sir. I remember the affair well—we had a lot of
requests at the time for photographs of both of them."

He came back presently with a profile photograph in his
hand—old, yellowing, a little dusty, one of a small pile tucked
away in the files.

It was Maximilian Golt all right. Loftus studied it for some
seconds, and Carruthers knew from the tightening of his lips
that he had found something at least of interest and perhaps of
importance.

Thanking the clerk, Loftus hurried back to the cab. He
gave an address in Jermyn Street, and ten minutes later the cab
drew up outside Thornton's flat. Loftus paid the cabby and
followed Carruthers, who had already pressed the bell.

A portly servant opened the door.

Thornton was one of the wealthiest of Craigie's men, many
of whom were apt to look on their Government pay as a
useful addition to a reasonably large income. Thornton's,
however, might be called even larger than reasonable. A
middle-aged man and the only son of a wealthy family, his flat,
a self-contained one on the ground floor, was the home of
objets d'art and Old Masters which were the envy of million-
aires. He had a collection of jade almost unique in England,
and was a connoisseur on many unexpected and rare subjects.

Well-known, and with the entrée to most political circles,
Thornton had gradually built up a position in which to

Craigie he was virtually invaluable while he remained unknown as a contact man. But after eight years his subversive activities were discovered, and he moved from Paris to London. Better that, Craigie had told him, than a knife in the back and another body found floating in the Seine.

Few in London suspected Thornton's part in the Secret Service.

Despite the hour—it was nearly one o'clock—Thornton was having breakfast. He jumped up from the table as they entered, his sad blue eyes sparkling.

"And what an honour! The great Bill himself, and before breakfast!"

"Don't you mean 'after lunch'," said Loftus laughing. "Don't stop for us, old son, we're only out for information."

"Ha! What's brewing?"

"What did you see of the man who went to Byng Court?" he asked, and Thornton said promptly:

"Part of his profile."

"Chin?"

"No, that was muffled up—quite naturally, I think, there was nothing furtive about the visit. I saw his mouth and nose, and his hat was pushed back on his head, so I know that his forehead slants a bit. Why?"

Loftus screened the photograph, so that only the nose, mouth and lower part of the forehead showed. He handed it to Thornton, who half-rose from his chair.

"Oh, yes. Not a doubt about it. That's the man."

"Good," said Loftus softly. "Very good indeed."

Only then did he begin to realise how important this latest discovery was—and it had sprung from the last expected source, from *La Reine*, who had a suite on the same floor of the Landon as the food directors. He did not let himself think much about that just then. He was too involved in the realisation that the man—whom he had believed important from the first—was known, and could easily be found.

"Who is it?" asked Thornton.

"Golt—a man named Maximilian Golt."

"So?" Thornton's years in Paris gave him at times a Gallic interrogatory manner. "*La Reine's* sponsor."

"You know that?" asked Loftus.

"In Paris she was the vogue," said Thornton simply. "We were all at her feet." He added with a humorous quirk: "She had a temper, and I doubt if age will improve it."

"Judging from Leroux of the Landon, it hasn't," said Loftus thoughtfully. "What do you know about Golt?"

"Nothing pleasant," said Thornton.

"Anything in particular?"

Thornton shrugged. "English, they said, although I was doubtful. He had the English accent well enough—rather rough, though, and uncouth. He might have been born here, but his ancestry . . ." Thornton shook his head. "Why all the interest in him, Bill? His record seems simple enough to me. He managed *La Reine* for a few years, they quarrelled and he went back to his circus."

"What?" Loftus almost shouted the word, and in that moment he felt a sharp sense of disappointment.

Thornton put a square of toast and marmalade into his mouth.

"*La Reine* quarrelled with everyone. The wonder was that she stayed with Golt for as long as she did. It was said in Paris that he had some hold over her other than influence, but then everything was said in Paris."

"Why didn't you recognise him last night?" asked Loftus.

Thornton shrugged.

"My dear Bill, it is eight—no, nine—years since I have seen

him, and then it was rarely. *La Reine* let him manage her, but she kept him in the background. He had no polish."

"Well, we haven't lost much time," said Loftus, "and we'll soon learn some more of Maximilian Golt. Have you seen anything of the Errols this morning?"

"Nothing," said Thornton.

Thornton's eyes lit up.

"What did you make of the woman at the Cherry?"

"Bill, I swear to you that she was a joy to look upon, and the loveliest creature I have seen for many years."

Loftus told him of Wally.

"Oh," said Thornton slowly, and he pushed his plate back sharply. "Why does he always get it? The injustice of it sickens me!" He stood up, striding the room, a quaintly impressive figure, his short legs enveloped in the folds of a scarlet silk robe embroidered with dragons. The others were silent as he went on: "Always it's the same. We can't start moving until murder has been done, before some of us are put out of action. Why *can't* we strike first?"

"Now, now," said Loftus gently.

Slowly Thornton's eyes lost their look of stormy tragedy. He shrugged his shoulders.

"Oh, I'm sorry. It gets me—it always does when one of the inside circle is hurt. But that's what we're for. Bill, have you ever realised that we—you, me, the others—have been at war for years? War isn't a new thing for us, we've never known peace."

Loftus said: "And probably never will. The world will be a better place when this war's over, please God, but there will still be unscrupulous bids for power, and so the threat of future war, bringing with it hideous and futile destruction. We'll have plenty to do," he added, and there was a quality of restraint in his voice which was impressive. "But it doesn't help us just now, Spats, to realise just how overwhelming are the forces arraigned against us. As soon as you're ready, chase round and find where the Errols are, and then phone me, will you?"

"Yes, of course. Any idea where they might be?"

"Probably at the Cherry or the like."

"Ah, ha! The beautiful damosel again," said Thornton roguishly. "I'll go there first."

"Right. Carry and I are off to see Craigie," said Loftus. He spoke hesitantly, however, and Carruthers knew that Oundle's continued disappearance was on his mind.

Before they went to Whitehall, Loftus walked to his own flat in the hope that Oundle was there, but the rooms were silent and empty.

In twenty minutes from the time of leaving Thornton's flat Loftus was making a full report to Craigie.

Until it was finished, Craigie made no comment, then he asked quietly:

"What made you think about Golt after you'd heard *La Reine* was at the Landon?"

"We-ell, all the people involved have been a little odd. There was the tiny girl, and the Shrimp with the unnaturally deep voice, and the dwarf at the Landon." He paused. "Quite a circus."

"Good Lord!" exclaimed Carruthers.

Craigie smiled.

"I don't think I would have seen it, Bill, but you told the Errols something about it, didn't you?"

"A hint or two," said Loftus. "I hadn't quite pieced it together then, but hearing of *La Reine* and remembering her early days, seemed to clinch it. In short . . ."

"We're dealing with a circus," finished Carruthers.

"I don't see any doubt about it," said Loftus crisply. "I think I ought to see Golt first, and *La Reine* afterwards. Right?"

Craigie nodded.

"And Carry can get to the Landon and keep an eye on the lady," said Loftus. "We've a line at last, thanks be, and a clear one. Will you get all the information you can on Golt, Gordon? This Myra Berne girl—she'll probably be connected with the stage or circus, and we might be able to blow them wide open in twenty-four hours."

"Is Golt likely to be the leader?" asked Craigie.

Loftus shrugged. "Who knows? He's a leader of sorts, anyhow. If it weren't for Wally and Ned we'd be feeling happy enough over the affair. I . . ."

He broke off, for one of several telephones on Craigie's desk rang sharply. Craigie lifted it, listened—and his knuckles went white as he gripped the instrument more tightly. He said "yes" three times at intervals, and then he replaced the receiver. His eyes were gaunt as he looked at Loftus.

"That was from Miller," he said. "They've found Ned in one of the empty flats, and the report's not good. He says he must see you, and he won't be moved until he has."

10

AND OF MYRA

L oftus lost no time.

The Bentley was parked in a small by-road, and Loftus automatically took the wheel. For all appearances he might have been unaware of Carruthers' presence, and the fair man knew that he was concerned only with two things. First, what news Oundle had; and second, what chance there was of Oundle recovering.

Carruthers hardly knew which would be the more important to Loftus's mind. In fact, Carruthers reflected in the short and fast drive to Brook Street, that none of them knew a great deal about Loftus's actual feelings. There were times when he appeared to be a perfectly normal man-about-town, when he enjoyed a night with friends yarning over the past and drinking copious quantities of beer. There were other times when he preferred to be on his own, and was not seen for days at a time. Yet his attitude towards his friends was always the same; even tempered, easily approachable, his emotions so well under control that it was impossible to gauge their depth or strength.

It was his ability to shut himself off from others, as he was doing in the car, which made Carruthers reflect that way, but there was not a lot of time for reflection. Loftus turned into Brook Street.

For the second time that day they saw an ambulance.

It was standing on the other side of the road, about three houses down from the Errols' flat.

Almost before the car had come to a stop Loftus was out of the Bentley and approaching the open front door of the house. By it stood a policeman—one of those who had been on duty outside the Errols' flat. The man saluted.

"Second floor, sir."

Loftus took the stairs three at a time. A plainclothes policeman, a uniformed constable, the sergeant who had been on the other side a while before, and a short, square-shouldered man with grey hair, turned at his approach. The doctor, thought Loftus.

Beyond them, he saw Oundle lying on a couch. His eyes looked enormous. They were wide open and the only touch of colour in his face; even his lips were colourless and it was clear that he was in considerable pain. The doctor spoke.

"Are you Mr. Loftus?"

"That's right."

"Can I have a word with you in private?"

"No. Say it aloud, please, you won't worry the patient."

A faint, very weary smile showed on Oundle's lips, but Loftus blessed the doctor, for he did not argue.

"It's simply this, Mr. Loftus—he is in great pain and he refused a morphia injection. It is necessary to make one quickly."

Loftus reached the couch. The thin man's lips tightened with a grimace of pain, but it passed. Sweat crept from his forehead down on to his face.

"Easy does it," Loftus murmured.

"Tummy trouble," Oundle said, and grimaced again. "The—grey bowler. Found him—here."

He paused, and there was a silence broken only by the two policemen leaving the room, and the doctor opening and closing his bag. Loftus rested a hand lightly on Oundle's shoulder.

"He was—on the phone," the sick man gasped. "Taking—orders. Called the other—Kay. Got that?"

"Yes," said Loftus.

"Had to—wait for you," said Oundle. "Daren't trust the others to get the message over." He talked very swiftly as the doctor stepped forward and Loftus nodded. The doctor pulled the blanket down, to show a bared arm. "I saw the bowler first. When I got here. Coming out of this door. He saw me reach Mike's place and dodged back. I came over. Back way. He was on his own—I thought. Heard him talking. Then someone else came in and let me have it. I got him—chest, I think."

"Time?" asked Loftus.

"I came straight here. Call it—ten minutes—after I got to the other flat." He tightened his lips again in a spasm of pain, but the needle had gone home with the shot of morphia, and it was not long before the lines on his face smoothed out a little. Loftus stayed there until Oundle at last closed his eyes.

Ambulance men were coming up the stairs.

"Well, Doctor," said Loftus in a curiously soft voice. "How long has he got?"

"They were small bullets," said the doctor. "Two of them—we might get him through."

"Get Bartlett," said Loftus, naming the foremost surgeon of the day. "He's done one job this morning already I hope, on another friend of mine. Tell him it's for Craigie—got that? Craigie."

"I'll arrange it," said the doctor.

Loftus nodded, and the doctor hurried down stairs.

Carruthers had been talking to the sergeant, and had taken the man's full report. Loftus looked pleased at that, and they walked across the road and to his own flat. There was a definite easing in the tension that had taken hold of Loftus; the possibility that Oundle would pull through seemed to be responsible for that. But he mixed a strong whisky-and-soda as soon as he reached the flat. Carruthers had not realised how pale he was until the colour flowed back to his cheeks.

"It wouldn't be a bad idea if we had some food," said Carruthers, and he telephoned the order to the restaurant that served many of the flats in Brook Street. That done he leaned back in an easy chair. Loftus was in another, toying with his whisky glass.

"What did the sergeant say?"

"Not as much as we'd like," said Carruthers. "He was searching the empty flats, when he found Ned crawling across the floor of one of them, trying to get to the telephone."

Loftus nodded. "He would."

"He didn't waste any time," said Carruthers. "The sergeant, I mean. He got Gordon's number for Ned and let him talk, and was getting the doctor and the ambulance on someone else's phone. Well, Bill, what's next?"

Loftus said: "We're really waiting on the Errols, and the Myra angle, but we'll get a *dossier* on Golt, *La Reine*, and an actress named Myra Berne. There should be a photograph of her at Arkeld's place—he might even have one in his wallet. Get all those things done, and see what Miller can do to help you. Ask him for a full report on the explosion. Oh, yes. A Greek named Letaxa and an American named Rannigan, were both staying at the Landon. See what you can find out about them, without letting them know.

"And then?" asked Carruthers.

Loftus smiled a little.

"You'll need some sleep," he said. "But there is another thing. Someone ought to go down to see Arkeld's secretary, in Bedford. Who've we got?"

"We-ll—Martin should be back."

"Try him," said Loftus.

A waiter brought their lunch. After he had laid the table and gone, Carruthers asked:

"What are you going to do?"

"First, to see Farrow, the servant at the Landon," said Loftus. "Second, to see *La Reine* if I can't get in touch with our Mr. Golt. Third—damn it, what does 'Kay' mean? Could be the initial or a Christian name or a surname, or even the name itself. That's another thing to talk to Miller about. See if it means anything to him."

"Right. What about the circus? Is Miller to start rounding that up? It will be Golt's lot, of course."

"Leave it," said Loftus almost sharply. "We don't want to disturb any of them yet. When we do, we'll start from the top. Let Golt think we're on the real track, and it will probably mean he'll stop using the stunt-merchants. For the time being it'll be enough to find out what we're up against."

Loftus left the flat first. There was no message from the Errols or from Spats Thornton. This was disturbing, but there was nothing he could do about it. He decided to seek out the address in Fulham of the servant Farrow. He hardly knew why he felt it was so important to see the waiter personally. It was a hunch and he was following it, not blindly but with his eyes wide open.

He drove his own car, a Talbot.

But he was worried when he reached Fulham, not because

he was followed, but because he was not. Why was no one following him?

"Answer that, and you'll answer a lot," he said to himself, and he slowed down outside the small terraced house in a street off New King's Road—the address of the waiter Farrow.

Mike Errol was unaware of tragedy.

He was, in fact, feeling at peace with the world, for his quest was a pleasant one, and offered no immediate danger— or so he thought. It was not difficult to remember Myra Berne, nor particularly difficult to go to the Cherry Club, which opened very early since the black-out virtually enforced an early closing-time.

He knew Anne, the attendant at the bar—not the blonde he had seen the previous night, but a short, dark, vivacious girl whom he privately thought should have found something better to do. She greeted him with a smile.

"You're early."

"I'm lonely, sweetheart. Are you always as empty as this in the morning?"

"And most of the day," said Anne.

"Oh, well, I had better have a drink."

"Isn't that what you've come for?"

He looked at her with a chuckle. "I'm not sure," he said, "but I think there's something going on in that pretty head of yours. I'll have a dry Martini, and you can tell me all about it."

She smiled as she mixed the drink.

"You made it pretty obvious last night, didn't you?"

"What, me?"

"She *was* lovely," said Anne. "*Is*, I mean."

"So it's got around, has it," said Mike gloomily. "I knew the day would come when you would find me out, darling, but I didn't think it would be so soon. What are you drinking?"

"It's too early, thanks."

"Principles or beauty conscious?"

Anne laughed: she was undoubtedly a pretty thing. She liked Mike Errol, and his cousin, and the men who came in and out with him from time to time. She thought wistfully how happy she would have been if it had been she who had been singled out by one of them and not Myra Berne.

She said abruptly: "Are you serious?"

"What about?"

She laughed a little awkwardly. "Why, Miss Berne of course."

"We-ell," said Mike thoughtfully, "if I thought there was a chance of getting past the others in the queue, I might think about it. But for the moment I'm just curious. How much can you tell me about her—I don't mean her morals."

"*They're* all right," said Anne unexpectedly.

"Are they, by Jove!" He played with his glass, but his eyes were serious as he looked at her. "Anne, I'm relying on you. They tell me that it's dangerous to rely on a woman, but I'm going to chance it. The lady—Myra Berne—seemed anxious to meet me last night. I heard a rumour that she was inquiring for me. Yes?"

"Grace told me so," said Anne. Grace was the blonde of the previous night.

"Does she come here often?"

"Well, quite often."

"Always alone?"

"Oh, no. It varies. She's with a man she calls Max quite a lot."

"What's he like?"

"Tall and dark—*I* don't like him."

"Nor do I," said Mike promptly, and she laughed. "Anyone else?"

The girl hesitated. "At one time she used to come here quite a lot—but only to meet someone."

"Pick-ups?"

"Oh, no. I've told you she isn't that type. She knew them all right, but they never left here together. She was on the stage, you know," she added.

"Was?"

The girl shrugged.

"She may still be acting in the provinces for all I know, though she's here too often to have a regular job with a touring company. The people she meets are certainly the stagey type."

"And that's all you can tell me about the lady?"

"If I can remember anything else I'll let you know."

"Good girl, and if she should come in, you'll tell her how interested I am and all that, won't you?"

"No, darling," said Anne shrewdly. "I won't. You know you can rely on me not to say anything."

"Not even to Grace."

"Not even to Grace. And I'm not going to ask you why you are asking so many questions . . ." she hesitated, and then broke off. Over the rim of his glass Mike looked into the mirror behind the bar.

In it he saw the reflection of Myra Berne entering the bar. The morning did nothing to disappoint a student of beauty. In fact he thought that she was, if anything, improved. She wore a dark, well-cut suit, her accessories were expensive, and in the best of taste.

Pausing for a moment by the door, it was clear that she, too, had seen a reflection in the mirror. It flashed through Mike's mind that she might decide to postpone the meeting, but she came on after a moment, and sat at the bar several stools away from him. He looked over and smiled.

"Good morning. What's it like out?"

She returned his smile. "A little warmer, I think."

"Oh, good." Mike stood up. "Have you a party coming, or can you drink with me? And please don't pretend you don't recognise me from last night." His smile was amiable, a little rueful, but in no way apologetic. "I was a little over the top, I'm afraid, but I've recovered to muse on my sins." He took the stool next to hers. Anne waited for the order.

"I'm expecting a friend," she said, "but thanks very much. May I have a dry sherry?"

"Good Lord!" exclaimed Mike. "A teetotaller!"

She had to laugh at him; people did. And when she laughed she showed her lovely white teeth. It occurred to Mike that she would be very pleasant to kiss.

"No, just temperate," she said.

Anne served them, and moved to the other end of the bar; he appreciated her discretion while he smiled into Myra's eyes, and said:

"Health and all that—not that you seem to need any more."

"More perhaps that you think," she retorted. She hesitated for a moment, and then added slowly: "You might, too."

"Good," he said. "Wish me all I need."

"I'm not sure that I want to," she said.

He looked as if he did not understand her. But he knew quite well that she was aware that he was interested in her, that she believed he had been following her, that he had been to Bedford. She deliberately gave him the impression that she knew of that, and he badly wanted to know why.

11

AN INVITATION

She drank slowly, keeping her eyes on him all the time. He continued to smile and to pretend that he had not taken the inference, although he wondered whether it was worth maintaining the pretence.

"We-ell," he said at last, "I suppose I'm still in disgrace over last night. A pity. As a matter of fact I thought I'd kept myself within bounds, but Mark . . ."

"Who is Mark?"

"My not-so-amiable cousin. He told me that I'd—oh, well, why go into that?" he demanded.

She looked at him intently.

"I wonder if you are just a fool," she said, and the directness of her words startled him. "Mr. Errol . . ."

"Hal-*lo!* But if I am to be known, why not as Mike?"

"You know that I know you," she said, speaking very quickly, "and was enquiring for you last night. What I'm not sure about is whether you realise quite how dangerous what you are doing might prove to be."

Mike chuckled.

"Danger and I travel together, my dear—didn't you know?"

"One day you might wish they didn't."

"I wouldn't say that," said Mike, and he wondered why she had decided to come into the open. It certainly looked as if her purpose was to warn him off, and that puzzled him. What he *was* sure of was the fact that she was far too curious about him, and in some way or other had learned too much.

Her voice grew sharper. "You're running yourself into needless danger."

"That it is needless I beg to question," he said.

She shrugged. "Play the fool if you want to. If you think it would be of any use, come and see me this afternoon. I can't talk here, I've friends coming at any time. They might not like to see me talking to you."

"Oh," said Mike, blank-faced.

"I don't want you to get hurt," she said hastily, and he could not be sure whether she was speaking the truth or whether it was part of whatever scheme there was in her mind. "You will be, you know, if you keep on with this—your friends have been already."

He frowned. "What friends?"

"You'll find out. Will you come?"

"Where is your flat?"

"You know as well as I do, it's 32 Byng Court. This afternoon at three o'clock."

He raised one eyebrow above the other.

"So I look as much of a greenhorn as that, do I?" he said. "My dear sweet Myra, if all you say is true, then the one place I don't come to is Byng Court, on my own that is. Actually, I . . ."

"Please yourself," she said swiftly, and he saw that she was glancing behind her. She moved very quickly, and reached a stool several removed from him as the door opened widely, and into the Cherry cocktail bar there stepped the tall, thick-set figure of Maximilian Golt.

Golt looked at Errol, then at the woman, as he stepped towards her, and began a low mutter of conversation. Mike ordered another Martini, drinking it at leisure. It would be wise, he thought, to follow them, but before that he wanted to get a word to Loftus. Loftus might have other ideas. The obvious thing for him to do was to get outside, phone from a call-box, and then wait until they came out. He was puzzled by her invitation. Although it held the marks of a trap, he wondered whether, if that were so, she would have adopted so obvious a device.

He finished his drink, and strolled out. There was a tele-phone kiosk fifty yards down the street, he knew, and he walked towards it.

But he did not go far.

Walking away from him quickly and in a manner which suggested she had been watching the Club and yet did not want him to see her, was the small creature who had outwitted the lot of them. He was quite sure it was the "child" whom Wally had brought to their flat, for she wore the same red beret and blue mackintosh.

He paused, thinking swiftly. It was possible that she there as a decoy, and if he followed her he might well be doing the wrong thing. But it was also possible that to follow her might be the right move.

And then round the corner, there came Spats Thornton.

Mike did not hesitate, but lengthened his stride. Spats and the girl passed each other, and then Mike met Spats, but did not stop. Out of the side of his mouth he spoke:

"Myra and boy-friend in the bar—boy-friend Max."

"Nice work. Bill's on to him," Thornton answered.

Mike sped onward, close on the heels of the "child". The

speed with which she walked was the most surprising thing about her. She went to Piccadilly, and then across the park, and occasionally she broke into a skip-and-run, as if filled with *joie-de-vivre.* Undoubtedly she played her part well, and he had to admire her for it.

Green Park—St. James's Park—Victoria Street—Victoria Station.

There she dodged him.

A weaving crowd was coming up from the tube station, and she merged into it. It was the last he saw of her, and after five minutes fruitless hunting he gave it up. He smiled ruefully. It was clear now that her mission had been simply to get him away from the Cherry.

He was prepared to admit that he was beaten. He could see no sense at all in the dodging, in Myra's manner, in her invitation, her apparent fear that the man called Max should see her with him. The fact that it did not appear to make sense did not mean there was none in it. He wished fervently that he could have five minutes' talk with Loftus.

"And there's no reason why I shouldn't," he thought.

He took a cab, instructing the driver to go to Brook Street. He did not appear to be followed, but to make quite sure he ordered the man to take a wide detour. None of the cars or taxis behind him turned off from the main road.

"Well, I'm quite alone," he decided. "I . . ."

But he was not as much alone as he had thought.

He did not see the car which came out of a side-turning until it was almost on him, and the driver was wrenching at his wheel. He had hardly time to be afraid before the car and car crashed, broadside on.

Mike had the sense to slide to the safer end of the cab. He did not entirely lose consciousness, but lay in a semi-stupor through which he heard the rending and the crashing about him. He found that he could not move, and after the first effort did not try, vaguely aware of a crowd gathering and the familiar and reassuring blue of policemen. After what seemed a long time, the wreckage was lifted from his legs and he was half-carried, half-dragged from the cab.

A doctor bustled up to the driver who had not escaped so easily, and lay waiting for an ambulance, then turned to Mike.

Very carefully he felt him all over and then, with a final prod, stood back.

"You're all right," he said. "A very lucky chap. There's nothing broken, but take it easy for a day or two." He bandaged a cut on Mike's hand swiftly and expertly, while the policeman, standing patiently by, took notes. Mike told him all that was necessary—which was virtually everything he knew.

"We'll get the driver all right, sir, he won't get far," the policeman said confidently. "How are you getting back, sir?"

"I'll take a cab," said Mike.

He was surprised to find that over half-an-hour had passed, and that it was two o'clock when he reached the flat. The policeman on duty there told him something of what had happened during his absence, but the fact that Loftus had been on the scene was reassuring. He went to Loftus's flat, and found no one there. He returned to his own, and telephoned the Westminster Hospital, giving Loftus's name and that of the patient as Davidson.

Whoever answered him said:

"It's too early to say anything about either of them, I'm afraid, Mr. Loftus."

"Either!" exclaimed Mike, and then he replaced the receiver, a much worried man. He cursed himself for not finding out who the second injured man was. It could be Mark, and he hated the thought of that. He was partly reassured by the sergeant who gave him the complete story—as he knew it.

It did not make Mike any happier—it looked as if the affair was bigger than he and the others had first thought. He wondered where Loftus was, and what he was doing. He rang Craigie, but there was no reply. He decided that the best thing he could do was to stay at the flat until someone or something turned up.

He wished very much that word would come from Mark.

In the house at St. John's Wood of the man who was known to some as Kay, the pleasant-looking youngster and the girl who had played the piano on the previous night sat talking in a room known as the office. Cabinets containing details of Kay's dealings in antiques, which he bought through agents, and bought keenly, lined the walls.

The girl was no more than nineteen or twenty, a light and fragile creature, to whom the young man had completely lost his heart and was by way of losing his head.

"I can't understand it," he was saying. "There's practically nothing to do here for either of us. When I came, he told me that he was always having trouble with his secretaries, and that for the right one he had plenty of work. I supposed . . ." there was a touch of bitterness in his voice as he went on— "that I was that right one, but it is beginning to appear that I am not."

The girl hesitated. "Why are you so bitter, Jim?"

"It's what life's made me," he said, with the dramatic exaggeration of youth. "Everything's gone wrong since I can remember—I even had to finish school a year early because the funds dried up. It isn't a lot of fun being entirely on your own, you know."

"It doesn't help to wallow. You take yourself and every-thing about you too seriously," she said.

It was surprising that so much common-sense was coming from one who looked so unworldly, but it did not occur to him as strange. He owed a lot to her practical suggestions in the month he had worked for the strange man with the short legs, known—though not to him—as Kay.

He frowned a little.

"It was when the war started that I had a really nasty kick. Nothing would go right—d'you know, Pam, I believe you're right! I began to feel sorry for myself then, that's why I felt so utterly fed up until I came here, and . . ." he smiled, a little shyly ". . . met you. It is sad that we don't have a lot of opportu-nity for talking."

She said: "We have it, but we don't take it. There's always a possibility that someone will overhear, and . . ." she shrugged.

"Do you feel that, too?" He looked startled. "I'd put it down to my imagination—but there is a queer kind of atmosphere here—as if we're always being watched."

She nodded. "We think they're all out now, but we can't be sure."

He pushed his hand through his hair.

"We'll hope they are, because now I've started to talk about myself I may as well go on, and maybe earn some more advice. Actually, Pam, it's like this. I didn't know my people—they were killed when I was an infant. There wasn't much money, and I was looked after by an aunt. Quite a dear, but very Victorian in outlook. I didn't really have a lot of affection for her, but it was a blow when she died. Then a year afterwards the money gave out, and I had to leave Charterhouse—Father was educated there, and Aunt had tried to see me through. Anyhow, I managed to get a job of sorts—office work wasn't attractive, but I was trained for nothing—and then came the series of crises, and jobs weren't easy to get. However, I managed." He grinned. "Then when the war came I tried to join the Air Force. They turned me down. Weak heart, they said."

Her face grew serious, but she said nothing.

"Then I tried the Navy and the Army—but it was always the same story. I suppose it all led to a grousing complex."

She nodded sympathetically.

They stood in silence for a moment. Then he went on: "I couldn't believe my luck when I was fixed up with him—he pays me pretty well, and I thought I was in clover. Then when I met you . . ." his voice shook a little. "One thing's quite certain—if he thought I was in love with his niece I would be flung out on my neck like a shot."

She laughed. "You're right, of course, but I don't think it would make a lot of difference in the long run. You'd like me to be honest, wouldn't you?"

"Of course. You know I would."

"He's had some really brilliant men, specialists in their subjects, and they've always gone after a month or two. I thought at first they annoyed him for some reason or other, but now . . ." she shrugged. "I don't think he wants to keep a secretary more than a few weeks. He fires them deliberately."

Jim Braddon stared. "But why on earth does he trouble to get them in the first place?"

She shrugged. "Who knows? He's an enigmatic man, not easily understood. During the interims he lets me keep his records straight. But not for long. He says I'm not strong enough."

She laughed, a light, silvery laugh that made her look unbearably lovely.

"I'm as healthy as a pony," she said, "and even tougher." She grew serious again. "I started this discussion because I thought

you ought to look for a job before he fired you. He will—I'm
quite sure of it."

Jim looked at her squarely.

"So it's like that. Did you do the same for the others?"

"No."

"Why did you pick on me?" He sounded gruff.

"Think it out," she said lightly. There was an undercurrent
of feeling in her voice which startled him. "I wouldn't want
you to stay—I don't want to stay myself. I've been here for six
years, and I was fresh from the country when I came. I knew
nothing and no one, and I was easily impressed. It's a
wonderful house, and I thought it was a palace. Well, perhaps
it is, but it's growing into a prison. I don't think I could get
away if I wanted to. When I go out I'm always driven by one of
the chauffeurs. When I go for a walk, there's always one of the
staff behind me. Haven't you noticed the same thing?"

"I—I hadn't given it a thought."

"Do, when you go out again," she said. "You'll be followed,
as I am. I sometimes think he's afraid that we're going to talk
about him. I think it's why he keeps changing his secretaries.
He's afraid they'll learn too much."

"About what?" demanded Jim, and he was perplexed as well
as startled. "All I do is keep records of antiques—there's
nothing else at all."

She shrugged. "I can't explain it, but I'd sometimes give a
fortune to get out of here—he scares me sometimes. He's not
really my uncle," she added casually. "I'm his ward. He gives
me as much money as I like, but—I'm not allowed to be
myself. It stifles me. Jim, get away soon, get a job somewhere
for me as well as you. I . . ."

She broke off abruptly, for from somewhere outside there
came the sharp ring of a door bell. Both of them looked
behind them, and neither spoke again.

Presently she heard her guardian climb the stairs and go into his study. She did not hear him walk to a cabinet and reach for a dictating machine. Nor did she hear her own voice and Braddon's faithfully repeated to him.

When the record was finished he spoke aloud but softly.

"That is a pity, a great pity. I was afraid one day . . ."

He stopped, stepped to his desk, and lifted the telephone, calling for Braddon. And then he waited with the tips of his long white fingers pressed together.

12
JOB FOR BRADDON

I t was a guilty conscience which made Braddon colour a little when he heard the summons. He did not delay in going to the study, and he hoped that his colour was normal when he tapped on the door, notebook and pencil in hand.

"Ah, Braddon." Kay spoke softly. "I don't need you for notes, at the moment. I have another task for you—one which will take you away for a few days." His eyes, so nearly black, did not move. "You have no objection to going out of London, I trust."

"Certainly not, sir."

"That is good. I want you to go to a house in Surrey—I will give you the address later, with full particulars. The address and instructions will be in a letter which you will have by three o'clock this afternoon."

"Very good, sir."

"You can drive a car?"

"Yes, sir."

"Good. A small Morris will be put at your disposal, and you will go to Guildford. Not until you are in Guildford will you open my instructions." The pale face smiled, but there was no humour in it. "That sounds mysterious, I have no doubt, but I want you to act on my instructions precisely."

"I will, sir."

"Be ready at three o'clock, then."

He nodded dismissal, and Braddon left the study with his mind confused. There was surely no possibility that the strange mission had been given to him because of his conversation with Pam? He frowned at the thought, then tried to laugh it aside. He could not. That uncanny feeling that everything he did and said in the house was seen or heard had been with him too long.

It had not occurred to him that what he did outside was also known.

Then, perhaps for the first time, he grew aware of a strange thing. Although he had never received instructions to stay indoors, it was rare that he went out. Occasionally he went to a theatre in the afternoon, or to a film. But somehow what little work he had to do always came at a time when officially he should have been free; it was as if he was deliberately prevented from having much spare time, particularly in the evenings.

He had not complained about that.

In fact he preferred to be at the house. There was the chance of Pam playing, or singing. All his thoughts revolved round her.

Not until that day had he fully realised how he felt towards the girl. And he smiled a little ruefully as he went to his office; she had been frank all right, and he was glad of it.

At three o'clock precisely he went for his instructions, received them, and was told to go to the garage immediately. He went downstairs and out of the back door, and then drew back, startled beyond measure.

Pam was sitting in a small Morris car, smiling at him.

"Well I'm damned," said Braddon clearly.

"I didn't know until ten minutes ago," she said. "I saw him at lunch, of course, and complained a little about being stuck in London. Then he said you were going to Guildford and would I like to go with you."

"And would you!" Braddon was suddenly in high spirits. To the girl it was a temporary respite from the stifling atmosphere of the house; to the man it was the prospect of two hours or more with her. With the additional joy of knowing that no one could overhear what they said.

But they were wary on the start of the journey.

They reached Putney and drove slowly towards Kingston, aiming for the by-pass. Deliberately they turned to scan the roads behind them, but they recognised none of the other cars, and twice there were long stretches of road completely empty.

Braddon looked at her happily.

"We're alone this time, all right. Let's forget him for a while."

Reaching Guildford he pulled up on the side of the High Street beneath the big clock, and took the sealed envelope from his pocket. He opened it slowly, to find another sealed envelope within marked clearly:

"Open as instructed."

On a slip of paper pinned to the envelope was a brief order to inquire at Guildford for Larch House, which was near the Farnham Road. They read the note twice, and Braddon said thoughtfully:

"Y'know, Pam, the reason for this mystery can only be that he wants to make sure that I can't tell anyone where I am going. Have you ever heard of Larch House?"

"No," she was as puzzled as he, but they lost no time in

making inquiries, and after three attempts they discovered a taxi-driver who was able to direct them.

It took them another half-an-hour to find the house. The sight of it did much to rob them of their high spirits.

For Larch House looked empty.

More than that; it gave the impression of having been empty for years. The drive was overgrown with weeds, unkempt bushes and trees pressing in from either side, all attraction of the small Georgian house itself nullified by neglect and dilapidation.

There was a warm sun above them, but it did little to lift the gloom. Pam shivered.

"What does it mean?" she asked.

"It's an odd business," said Braddon, but he pulled up outside the house, and opened the door. "Will you stay here while I have a look round?"

"Oh, no, I won't stay by myself, I'll go with you."

"Scared?"

"In a way, yes. I don't like it. Do you?"

"We-ell—it's certainly puzzling," he said. "If we didn't know him better I'd say it was a practical joke. We'll try the front bell, anyhow."

As they stepped to the porch they could see through the windows of the room on the right. The window was dirty, and one pane was broken and covered with cardboard, but the room was furnished, the chairs covered with dingy dust sheets.

"I like it less and less," said Pam. "I—oh, what's that?"

"That" was a bell which pealed out close to them, and echoed loud about their ears.

"That's odd," Braddon said, after a moment, "the bell's been oiled recently." He looked at a smear of oil on his glove, and then they both started, for they heard footsteps coming along the hall.

A fat man opened the door, and anyone less likely to be in that house it was impossible to imagine. He was very fat—so fat that he seemed unreal. He wore a grey bowler hat, and an over-tight check suit. His voice, when he spoke, held the brassy quality of one used to being heard above a din.

"Hallo there. Come right in both of you—I've been expecting you."

Braddon conceived a sudden and sharp dislike of the man, while Pam looked round in growing dismay at the thick dust on the boarded floor. She clutched Braddon's sleeve. "Open the other envelope, Jim," she urged.

"You don't have to worry about that," said the fat man. He snatched the envelope out of Braddon's hand. "You don't look as if you like it both of you. Pity, since you're going to stay here quite a bit. Upstairs, young fellow-me-lad."

Pam thought that Braddon would hit him.

It made her afraid. She knew suddenly that her conversation with Jim had been overheard, and this was the answer. She was afraid that Braddon was going to start a fight, and she knew that he would be helpless against the fat man.

But Braddon did not start it. He had no chance, for as if from nowhere a dwarf leapt at him and aimed a blow at the back of his knees. Pam cried out as Braddon fell to the ground but the sound did no more than echo about the almost empty house, while the fat man seized her wrist. His fleshy fingers had a surprisingly powerful grip.

"Don't you start," he said roughly, and he began to push her towards the dusty, uncarpeted stairs.

Meanwhile Loftus had interviewed a man named Farrow.

Loftus had wondered several times whether his hunch was a good one, for Farrow had not been at home when he had first arrived, and he had waited, in a small, over-furnished front room for half-an-hour.

The man entered at last, with the stiff, flat-footed walk of an elderly waiter.

"Good morning, sir. What can I do for you?"

Loftus smiled.

"I'm not sure that you can do any more than you have already," he said. "It's about the business at the hotel."

"I see, sir." Farrow's eyes gazed at him without expression. "I gave a full story to the police, and signed a statement."

"Let me have the gist of it, will you?" asked Loftus.

"Certainly, sir. May I see your authority?"

"Of course." Loftus took out a card signed by the Assistant Commissioner of Police, Sir William Fellowes, and by the Home Secretary. Farrow read it and handed it back.

"Thank you, sir. Roughly, what happened was this: Mr. Rannigan, an American gentleman, frequently rings for refreshment during the night. I am the night waiter."

"Refreshment?"

"It is usually tea, sir, although sometimes he prefers minerals."

"I see. Go on, please."

"His bell rang about five minutes to twelve, sir, and I telephoned him—as previously arranged—and he ordered tea. Water was boiling, sir—we always have it available, and I was able to take it along at once. I went up the main stairs, and could not have been more than five or six minutes."

"Good. Go on."

"I took the tea in, and placed it on his bedside table. He acknowledged it, and I went out. As I closed the door I heard the shot—or what might have been a shot. I waited for some seconds but I heard nothing else, so I went downstairs."

"I see," said Loftus. "You didn't raise any alarm?"

"No, sir."

"You weren't sure what it was, I suppose?"

"I hadn't a great deal of doubt, sir. I served through the last war, and one gets used to shooting. But it might have been an accidental shot—several officers are staying at the hotel, and there are accidents in cleaning. I thought it best to say nothing—any undue disturbance at night would have been unfortu-nate, sir, and jobs aren't easy to get in the trade these days."

"I suppose not." Loftus's eyes gleamed humorously. "Manager a bit of a tartar, eh?"

Farrow smiled but did not commit himself.

"Do you know which room it came from?" asked Loftus.

"I'm afraid I can't help there, sir. I *thought* it came from the first floor, but as I knew no army officers had their rooms there, I told myself I had made a mistake."

"I see. No one else heard it, as far as you know?"

"I haven't been told so, sir. Mr. Rannigan didn't, or he would have called me—he dislikes noises at night, and had a special fitting made to his door to render his room as quiet as possible. *Madame La Reine* would, I think, have complained had she been disturbed."

"Who?"

"*Madame La Reine,* sir, the actress. I don't know her real name."

"I see. And you've no idea which room the shot came from?"

Farrow raised his brows interrogatively.

"I thought it was known to have been from Mr. Arkeld's room, sir. I was given to understand that by the manager."

"Just a formality," Loftus said easily. "And there's nothing else you can think of that might help?"

"I'm afraid not, sir."

"No quarrelling? No gun anywhere?"

"No, sir."

"Oh, well," said Loftus. "I suppose I can't expect too much, and your summary, like your report, is admirably concise. Thank you, Farrow."

"I'm glad to be able to help, sir."

Loftus climbed into his car and let in the clutch as the door closed. He drove thoughtfully for five minutes, and then pulled up outside a telephone kiosk. He was lucky in finding Miller in.

"Loftus here," he said, and without preamble: "Have a man put on Farrow, will you? A really good one."

"Certainly," said Miller. "May I ask why?"

"Because he's a waiter who is afraid of losing a job; also because he has a gold cigarette lighter, and a pretty expensive suit. He may or may not get big tips, and there could be a perfectly good explanation of it—but it's curious, and he should be watched. Check up his history, too, will you?"

"Ye-es," said Miller, and it seemed as if he laughed. "You do get ideas, don't you," he added. "Have you heard anything else?"

"Not enough," said Loftus. "But I'd like to see a man named Golt—Maximilian Golt. How quickly can you look up his address for me? It's probably in London."

"If you phone me in five minutes I'll have it," promised Miller, and he was as true as his word. From a kiosk at Victoria Loftus made the second call, and was told that Maximilian Golt lived in a block of mansion flats in Putney. He had two telephone lines, one of them "ex-directory", which meant that the number was not in the telephone book. He had lived at the same address for at least three years.

"Good," said Loftus. "I think I'll have a word with the gentleman. Has anything else come in?"

Miller said quietly: "Yes, the analyst's report on the blood. That on the pillow is Group A, Arkeld's is Group B."

"Hmm," said Loftus thoughtfully. "It helps, and it complicates. One way and the other we're having a nice time, aren't we? Keep checking all you can at the hotel, and I'll get in to see you some time this afternoon."

Loftus rang off, returning slowly and reflectively to his car. He had started the engine when he heard his name called, and looking round he saw Mike Errol drawing up behind him.

13
LOFTUS SAYS "YES"

In the first glance over his shoulder Loftus saw nothing of Mike's bandaged hand, nor of the dust on his clothes, and a tear some five inches long in the leg of his trousers. But as he braked and Mike stepped alongside, the damage was obvious. Loftus raised an eyebrow.

Mike grinned, and plunged forthwith into a recital of what had happened.

Having finished the early part of his report, and described the accident, he went on:

"So I phoned Miller, learned Farrow's address, and came down in the hope of picking you up, old man. Before the car business I think I would have gone off on my own to see Myra, but now—well, what do you think?"

"I think yes," said Loftus promptly.

"Alone?"

"Don't you feel like it?"

"Don't be an idiot," said Mike mildly. "I don't give a damn whether I go alone or with an army. We can only die once. But if anything does happen to come my way and I'm alone, it might be awkward."

"We-ell," said Loftus, scratching his chin, "it's a question of the lady's sincerity. It is possible that she and Golt have fallen out, and if that's the case then she might have some information for you. But if she has any idea that you're not alone, then she's likely to close up. I think I'd chance it."

"Right," said Mike briskly. "And as it's just on three, I'd better get a move on. I don't think I'll change. If I turn up like this it might give added point to something or other—I'm not quite sure what, but it might."

Loftus smiled. "You may have a point there. What have you managed to find out for me?"

"Not a lot," said Mike. He had telephoned Miller. There was no photograph of Myra Berne at Arkeld's hotel, nor in his wallet, but Mike had a small Leica. He proposed fixing it to his waistcoat so that he could take a variety of snaps that afternoon.

"Good," said Loftus.

"Miller's getting all the dope on *La Reine*, the Greek, Rannigan and whatnot," said Mike. "And I telephoned Martin Best—he's on the way to Bedford now to see this secretary, Arkeld's girl. That's the lot, I think."

Loftus sighed. "About one third of the lot. The food directors and associates are still at the Landon. Some of them think that there was an attempt to exterminate them by today's explosion."

"So you agree with them?"

"Not necessarily," said Loftus. "But Arkeld was certainly murdered, and Mortimer and the others could well be. There's a bunch of Special Branch men looking after them for the time being, and I don't think there's any immediate danger. Have you heard from Mark?"

Mike shook his head.

"Hmm," said Loftus. He brooded for a moment, and then went on: "You deal with Myra, and I'll get on to Golt's tail. I want to scare that gentleman, and in any case I'll . . ." he paused, as if suddenly seized with a completely new idea. "Mike, get to your flat and wait there until I phone. Phone Myra yourself, and tell her you'll be late."

"Now what's the idea?" demanded Mike with some resignation.

"A simple one. I'll make sure Golt's in before you go. If he's not, he might turn up at Myra's flat and that wouldn't help you."

"Right." Mike leapt into the Bentley, and set off.

But Loftus did not immediately go to the flat of Maximilian Golt.

He pulled up outside a kiosk on the Surrey side of Putney Bridge, and telephoned Craigie. To introduce himself he used a code which had been used for years in the Department, and had never been misused. He gave his name, and then began to spell it backwards. As he reached "f" Craigie's quiet voice said:

"All right, Bill."

"Anything?" asked Loftus.

"Ned and Wally came through the operation all right, and the chances are still fifty-fifty," said Craigie.

"Good work." There was no emphasis in Loftus's words. "I'll be back in an hour or so, I hope, but meanwhile there's another thing. Mike's on the way to see Myra, and he's going alone—or he thinks he is."

"Well," said Craigie, "Mark telephoned from Golders Green ten minutes ago, and he's coming here to report."

"Good! Get him there," said Loftus. "To the siren's flat, I mean. Tell him not to show himself, will you, and not to let Mike have any idea he's about. If it is a set-up, then the place will be watched closely when Mike goes in, and if he's apparently quite alone there might be interesting developments."

"Right," said Craigie. "I'll phone Mark for you."

"Thanks. Nothing else?"

"Nothing that can't keep," said Craigie, and he rang off.

His words intrigued Loftus, but did not worry him. Had the "something which could keep" been of great importance he would have been told about it. He suspected that it was something to do with Mortimer, or even Hershall—probably Mortimer had been making himself felt in Whitehall. There was the difference of opinion amongst the members of the conference to be taken into account, he reflected. He wished that he could give them fuller attention, but the opportunity was not there for the time being.

He drove on to Fairway Mansions, an imposing block of modern flats on the top of Putney Hill.

He pulled into the carriage-way.

La Reine and Rannigan puzzled him, and he was put in mind of them by the reflection on the number of people who stayed in London, braving the threat of raids, when there was no need. It was difficult to imagine a less likely place for an old American—who was also an invalid—to convalesce. Yet that was precisely what Rannigan was attempting to do. Moreover, he was so touchy about noise that he had a specially made protection fitted to his door.

In normal times it would have been understandable.

In these days it was incredible. A dozen padded doors would not keep out the sound of bombs, or of A.A. fire. It was an inconsistency which had crystallised his interest in the unknown American.

Letaxa, the Greek, had a mission in London, and his presence was understandable. But *La Reine* gave him a problem which stuck out a mile.

She had been staying safely in the country, yet she had returned to London where, if Leroux had told him the truth, she was proposing to remain for the rest of the summer. It was hard to believe that the actress would do that willingly. According to reports she had saved a great deal, and it was even rumoured that she was one of the wealthiest people in the profession. What, then, was the reason of staying in town where bombing was a virtual certainty?

The first floor at the Landon, reflected Loftus as he stepped into Fairway Mansions, should be able to tell us a lot. He glanced at a note he had made of Golt's number, and saw that it was 32. Odd, that. The fact that the number was the same as Myra Berne's at Byng Court had escaped him when he had first heard it from Miller. He tucked the coincidence to the back of his mind, and went up the lift without speaking to the hall porter.

Number 32 was on the second floor.

He discovered that he had to turn two corners before he reached it, and he was approaching the second when he heard a door open somewhere ahead of him, and then the sound of voices. One was so clear and unmistakable that for a moment Loftus stood quite still, wondering whether he had heard aright.

Then he moved.

There was a house-maid's cupboard near him, and he opened it and slipped inside.

Footsteps passed him.

As they faded, he stepped back into the passage, and followed the man whose voice had been so familiar. He saw the stocky, broad-shouldered figure of Mr. Daniel Fortescue, the north-country regional director of food distribution.

A second later Loftus saw that there was only one flat from

which he could possibly have come. *It was the flat of Maximilian Golt.*

There was a popular daily paper which had for some reason or other decided to play Fortescue up strongly, and for weeks the activities of "Honest Dan" had been prominently displayed in the *Daily Echo.* This, Loftus now recalled. It was difficult to imagine a man whose appearance answered the description of "Honest Dan" more compellingly than Fortescue's; but his presence at Golt's flat opened an immense vista of possibilities.

But it was too early to jump to conclusions.

It was also too early to visit Golt. The man would know that there was a chance that his earlier visitor had been seen, and that might cause unnecessary trouble. Loftus therefore waited five minutes before ringing the bell of Golt's flat.

There was a short pause before the catch of the door was slipped back. That it had been necessary to slip it forward suggested that Golt was aware of the possibility of someone trying to force an entry.

Golt opened the door.

"Well?" His voice was harsh.

"Good-afternoon," said Loftus, and he smiled in a fashion which had often served to disperse suspicion of his intentions. Apparently it did not impress Golt, who continued to stand squarely in the doorway, his expression both forbidding and impatient. Loftus took in the slanting forehead, the high-bridged nose. The mouth and chin were more than unpleasing; they were both coarse and brutal, proclaiming that here was a dangerous man with little or no respect for ordinary human scruples.

"Can you spare me five minutes, Mr. Golt?" asked Loftus mildly.

"No, I'm busy."

"Not too busy to hear what I have to say, I hope."

Loftus moved forward, and Golt drew back a hand as if to resist him. He changed his mind at the last minute, and stepped grudgingly aside.

"What the devil does this insolence mean?" snapped Golt.

"I hardly know," said Loftus, mildly. "Can it be that I'm not recognised?"

"I don't know you from Adam!"

Loftus took out his wallet and extracted a card—which declared him to be a member of the Special Branch at Scotland Yard.

Golt stared at it impassively.

He was putting up a good show, thought Loftus. Would it be possible to break him down?

"Pity you didn't show me this before you pushed your way in," Golt said, a little less sharply. "Well, now you're here what d'you want?"

Loftus spread his hands with a bland show of honesty and regret. "Mr. Golt, there is no purpose in beating about the bush—you'll be the first to agree with that, I'm sure. You have been known to associate with people whose interests are considered inimical to the safety of the state."

Golt stared at him, and for some seconds did not speak. When he did he turned away sharply, and his eyes evaded Loftus's.

"Nonsense," he said gruffly. "You should know me better."

"Now come," said Loftus. "I haven't time to waste on anything that can be dismissed as easily as that. I want to make sure of your connection with these people."

"Who are they?" Golt was standing his ground well,

reflected Loftus, and yet in those much-veined eyes there was a hint of apprehension which suggested that the man was worried.

"A Miss Myra Berne, for one," said Loftus.

Golt stared at him, and then suddenly he laughed. It was not a pleasing sound. Before he had quite finished he stepped back and sat on the arm of a chair.

Loftus eyed him calmly.

"You are amused?"

"Good God!" exclaimed Golt. "What next will you blasted officials be up to? Myra inimical to the State!" He went off into another peal of laughter, and Loftus knew that the cause of it was because Golt was relieved. "I've known her for years —she once acted in one or two plays I put on. She hasn't anything to do with politics—and only enough brain to choose a frock."

"I hope you're right," said Loftus. "Have you seen her lately?"

"Yes—this morning, and for that matter last night." He laughed coarsely. "If you want to know my relations with the lady, remember I'm a producer and she's an actress who wants to get on, and make three guesses."

There was little that Loftus liked about Maximilian Golt, but at that moment he had a strong urge to kick him. He conquered the urge, and continued to eye Golt calmly.

"When had you seen her before last night?"

"Not for some weeks."

"Are you *quite* sure?" demanded Loftus.

"Yes, I am." It might have seemed surprising that Golt was prepared to answer the questions so freely, but Loftus did not find it so. He knew that Golt believed he understood the full reason for the call, that Golt was confident there was no way in which he could be implicated. "She's been down to her cottage near Bedford. She isn't mean with her favours," he said, and the sneer was back again. "She's been playing around with a man named Arkeld, but they had a row, and she came back last night."

"I see," said Loftus gently.

He admired the other's tactics dispassionately. Myra was suspect of some part in Arkeld's murder, and he, Golt, was known as an intimate friend of Myra's. It was natural that the police would make inquiries, but there was no reason why they should—as yet—suspect Golt himself. Loftus considered for some seconds, and then smiled, giving the impression that he was satisfied. He took his cigarette-case from his pocket and proffered it. Golt accepted one, and as a match flared Loftus said:

"Look here, Golt, I'll be frank with you. It is the association with Arkeld that is giving us trouble. Have you any reason to believe that Miss Berne's association with him was anything other than amorous?"

Golt's eyebrows drew together.

"*Was* anything?" he said.

"Arkeld died last night," said Loftus briefly.

Golt stood up sharply.

"My God, now I see what's worrying you. I—but Loftus, I can assure you that she was interested in him only from the er— amorous angle, yes. Actually he's very generous, you know, and she's a lovely woman. I thought at one time that some-thing serious would come of it, and I was surprised to hear from her again yesterday. I won't say I'm sorry, but . . ." he shrugged his shoulders, and his manner was that of one man-of-the-world to another. Loftus had the urge to kick him again; there was something obscene about this uncouth-looking man adopting the "good-fellow" air. "Well, you know what I mean," Golt added. "I'm quite sure you're on the wrong line when you worry about Myra."

Loftus smiled. "That's helpful, anyhow. I wish I hadn't had to trouble you, but these are difficult days."

"Yes, indeed," said Golt. "They give you policemen johnnies quite a free hand, too, don't they? Oh for the happy days of peace!" He suggested a drink.

Loftus refused, thanked him, took up his hat and left.

He did not know it then, but he made a mistake which might easily have proved fatal. For had he waited another five minutes he would have seen the man who was known to some as Kay. As it was he saw the Daimler which was pulling into the carriage-way as he drove out. He saw also the pale-faced, distinguished-looking man in the tonneau, a man who stared at him and then away, but he thought nothing of it. Had he seen the little legs he would have been at least interested, for the legs made Kay a freak, and Loftus was interested in freaks—particularly those which might play some part in a circus.

Kay was driven up to Fairway Mansions, and went to Flat 32.

Loftus drove back towards London, pondering on Maximilian Golt and the likely effect of the call.

14
STRANGE STORY

Golt opened the door to his third visitor when Kay's hand was hardly on the bell. He stood aside as the older man stepped through, but their eyes met, Golt's hot and out of temper, Kay's cool and appraising. Kay chose a low chair with care, and said quietly:

"I saw Loftus coming away from here."

"I was dead scared he would see you," said Golt, breathing heavily. There was both anxiety and an undercurrent of satisfaction in his voice, as he went on: "I handled him all right, though, don't worry about that."

"Are you sure?"

"Quite sure." Golt lit a cigarette and flicked the match towards the fireplace. "He came to find what he could about Myra. He told me that Arkeld was dead and wanted to know what there was between him and Myra—was it just 'amorous'!" Golt laughed again, his mouth very wide. "I milk-fed him all right—but when he first came I thought he had something on me."

"Ye-es," said Kay. "That would worry you."

"Wouldn't it you?" snapped Golt.

"Perhaps. So you feel sure that he was merely trying to find whether Myra gained information from Arkeld—is that it?"

"I'm dead sure," said Golt confidently. "I would have seen if there was anything else behind it, don't worry. But I had a scare—Fortescue had only been gone five minutes."

Kay said softly: "The timing of Loftus's visit was remarkable, wasn't it?"

"Just a coincidence," said Golt, comfortably. He went on to discuss the call of Daniel Fortescue, and what had transpired. They talked for fifteen minutes, and then Kay stood up and reached for his hat.

"It should be satisfactory, Golt. Tonight, of course, will tell us more. I have all the arrangements made for the series of—er—disasters, or so, I have no doubt, the Government will call them. And the Press, if they should reach the Press. If they should not . . ." he laughed that silent laugh of his, but his eyes were deadly sober as he looked at Golt. "We shall look after that, of course. Now there is one other thing. It has been necessary for me to send my niece and my secretary away for a few weeks. There is no longer any need for you to watch them."

Golt stared. "Where are they?"

"At Larch House. Barker is looking after them. You will see him later in the day, and you will remind him that Pamela is not to be ill-treated, but is to be made as comfortable as possible. I did not like the need for putting her there, but she is a woman—and curious," he shrugged. "You will be very definite with Barker. He has peculiar ideas. Loftus used the word—amorous. It describes him. Pamela is on a short holiday, but she must not be put to any unnecessary inconvenience. You understand?"

"Yes, I'll tell him," said Golt.

"I trust you will," said Kay, and he stepped towards the door with absurdly small steps. Golt did not follow him along the passage. Shutting the door, he flung himself on to a settee. His hands as he lit a cigarette were not entirely steady.

So the old man had found it necessary to send the girl away. That meant he was worried—he was fond of the kid, and he would not have taken any steps about her unless he knew that there was acute danger. The secretary didn't matter, but the girl . . .

Golt shrugged, but it was a fact that he was more worried by Kay's call than by Loftus's, wherein he made a mistake—not the first of his interesting career. He thought of Myra—they were on to Myra all right, and she would be useless in the future. He wondered what Kay would do about that. Skippy had been killed; it would be a pity if Myra had to go too.

Golt squashed out his half-finished cigarette, and a few seconds afterwards lit another. He was worried because he knew that Kay did not tell him everything, not even half of it.

He hoped to God that he himself was in the clear.

Loftus returned to Whitehall, and went immediately to see Craigie. As he reported what had taken place, Craigie's expression lost much of its cheerfulness.

"The man is more clever than we thought, Bill."

"He put it over well enough," admitted Loftus, "although I helped him. He's now convinced that the trouble is likely to come through the woman. So we ought to watch her very closely. Mike hasn't reported?"

"No, and there's nothing from Mark."

"I hope they're not too long," said Loftus, and for a moment his expression was sombre. "I don't like it when anyone is overdue in this show. Have you heard from Miller?"

"He's sent over a full report," said Craigie. He passed a copy to Loftus. It was comprehensive and interesting, but no more. The essentials were:

Martin K. Rannigan. American drug-store owner with a widespread chain. Dollar millionaire. Spent last three years in France—Riviera. Came to London before the fall of France. Spent the winter in Cornwall. Returned to London early in April. Known to be under medical care, believed to be for valvular disease of the heart. Reputation excellent. Inquiries being made in New York. American Embassy give unqualified reference.

Madame Yvonne de Bourcy—known as La Reine. Musical comedy actress of renown. Career commenced as circus performer. Associated with Maximilian Golt for fifteen years until 1936. Married in 1927 to Jules de Bourcy, who died in 1931. Political activities—none known. (There followed details of her stay in the country and in London, as already known to Loftus. The only possible point of interest was that she had stayed for the winter in Devon.)

Maximilian Golt. Stage-manager and producer, once circus owner. Interested in a chain of provincial theatres. Interested in Barker's Circus, which broke up soon after outbreak of war. Political associations unknown.

* * *

Arthur Farrow. Waiter at Landon Hotel. Been there for three months. References from several London hotels now being checked. Little known of private life.

Loftus read the reports a second time, and then glanced at Craigie with a look of inquiry.

"Could Miller give us anything about the Greek?"

"Oh, I forgot that. He's conferring with the Greek Embassy before he sends a report, but as far as he knows there's nothing against the man."

"We-ell," said Loftus, "that seems to see us through, and offers possibilities of further developments. The next thing is to wait for Mike and Mark, I suppose. Did you send anyone else there?"

Craigie smiled. "I don't think anyone will get out, Bill, without being followed."

"Good work, then I'll get back to the flat, and try to work things out." Loftus walked over to the sliding door, pausing before he set it in motion. "What was it that could wait?"

Craigie looked a little rueful.

"Hershall came through. Apparently Mortimer asked for special protection, and is generally making a nuisance of himself. Hershall wanted to know what the devil we were doing."

Loftus chuckled.

"Mortimer might be a lot more of a nuisance if he knew where Fortescue was this afternoon—and that gives me an idea. An S.B. man should have followed him. Supposing we ring Miller and find if any report's come in?"

One had, and it was not a good one. A Special Branch man detailed to watch Fortescue had followed the Lancastrian from

the Landon to Victoria, and then lost him. There was a vague-
ness about the report which Miller had not liked. He had questioned the agent, who admitted that a child had cannoned into
him while he had been watching Fortescue, and when he had
picked himself up the director had been nowhere within sight.

Loftus laughed grimly. "That 'child' is doing a lot of good
work for the other side, Miller. But it doesn't matter now."

It did matter, however, in as far as Fortescue's visit to Golt
would have been unknown had Loftus's call not coincided
with his: and Loftus reflected that the sooner one or the other
of them made a point of watching Fortescue the better it
would be.

Loftus, of course, had no idea of what was portending for
that night.

Nor did Mike Errol.

It was nearly four o'clock when he eventually reached
Byng Court, and rang the bell of Number 32. It was opened by
a maid who, after two or three minutes, looked into the
lounge where Myra had greeted him and asked whether she
was wanted again. She was dressed then for out-of-doors.

Myra had said "no."

Mike Errol was in two minds as to his attitude, although
when he had entered the lounge he had found it difficult to
keep from laughing.

The scene was nicely set, he had reflected, for seduction.

Warmth, beauty, an invitation to repose—it was all there,
even to Myra's half-revealing, half-concealing gown.

But there was no doubt that she *was* lovely.

He did not think that he had seen a lovelier creature. But
he had thrust the personal issues aside quickly, and had let
Myra start the talking.

"Mike," she said at last, after ten minutes frothy chatter, her voice deepening to seriousness, "if things were different we could be good friends."

"Yes, couldn't we!" he said.

"Why do you think I asked you here?"

He chuckled, and tapped the ash from his cigarette.

"Quite honestly I'm expecting the door to open at any time and my executioner to appear."

"Why come alone, then?"

"That was the understanding, wasn't it?"

"And you ignored the risk?"

"I wouldn't quite say that," said Mike, "but while we're on the subject, tell me *why* you asked me here."

Cool, appraising eyes watched him between lowered lids.

"It could have been because I wanted your company."

"Oh, yes," he said politely, "it could have been."

"It could even have been because I wanted to warn you not to continue to be foolish," she went on.

"As a matter of fact, that's my bet," said Mike Errol. "Ensnared by the charm of whatever there is charming about me, you decided that I should be rescued from the fate which traditionally awaits Nosey Parkers."

"*Can't* you talk sensibly?" Her voice was sharp.

He looked at her for a moment, and then he deliberately stood up, and stepped towards her. She did not move, nor did she protest when he sat down at her side, and slid an arm about her shoulders. With his free hand he arranged a cushion so that he could be comfortable, and still look at her.

"What do we want with common-sense?" he asked softly. "It's a short life, my dear. But now we're comfortable, let's see what we can do about talking sensibly. You start. Why were you asking for me?"

"I wanted to know why you followed me in Bedford."

"How do you know it was I who followed you?"

"That doesn't matter."

"All right," he said. "Let's start again. What do you know about me?"

She had to turn her head a little to stare into his eyes, and he thought that she was wondering whether to tell the truth or whether to lie to him. Beyond that he could form no opinion about her, or the reason for the invitation. It was certainly not for the chance of an *affaire*. Anne of the Cherry had said she wasn't the type, and despite his knowledge of her association with Arkeld and with Golt, he was inclined to agree with her. She gave him the impression that she could be as unattainable as the stars—if she so wished it.

She said clearly:

"Your name is Michael Errol, you have independent means, you live with a cousin who is so much like you that you are often taken for twins. You appear to do nothing useful but you are often away, and surprising things happen in and near your flat from time to time. You have been watching Sir Thomas Arkeld for some days, you grew interested in me, and soon transferred your attentions to me. You followed me from Bedford to London, and you went to the Cherry Club last night to meet me, or at least to see me. Am I wrong?"

Mike was inwardly perturbed, outwardly amused.

"Well, I could sketch in the details," he said. "I had a look through that charming cottage of yours, and covered you with a tablecloth . . ."

"So that was you, was it?" she said, and he knew that she was laughing at him. He was not pleased, but he said lightly:

"Guilty. And I didn't go to the Cherry Club to meet you, I went by accident. Last night, that is. But how have you managed to get all this information, sweetheart?"

"The means are immaterial," she said lightly, "but the fact that I have this information should really be enough to warn you."

He pursed his lips. "Perhaps. But haven't we rather strayed from the original point which is: 'Why did you invite me?' "

"I wanted to tell you to go away." She leaned forward. "Mike, don't go on with whatever you're doing."

"It's necessary, I'm afraid," he said slowly.

"Necessary!" Her words held a touch of bitterness. "You'll throw your life away, like others have done, like Arkeld did . . . "

She stopped abruptly, the colour fading from her cheeks as she watched him. But she did not try to evade his eyes, and he watched her soberly for some seconds. When he spoke his voice was dry and expressionless.

"So you knew he was dead."

She tried to speak, but the words either would not come, or were deliberately stopped. Her manner was so natural that he could not reach a decision easily. He could see no purpose for a sincere talk, for a genuine warning; the subject of what she was did not ring true, but the manner did. And to support the theory of sincerity there was her slip—if slip it was, and not deliberate, about Arkeld.

She said roughly:

"Well, what are you going to do now?"

"I don't quite know," said Mike Errol. "I wish I could make up my mind as to your real motive."

She looked at him quickly, and something in her expression told him that he was wrong to trust her. But he could not see the trap, he had no idea what she wanted him to do.

Was she waiting for someone?

He said: "If this business were finished, what would you think about me?"

"What use is there in thinking about it," she said fiercely.

133

"This business as you call it isn't finished, in any case. I suppose you're worried because there was trouble in Arkeld's food area."

"How did you know that?"

"Because he told me—he was worried enough himself, for the last two or three weeks. He was even frightened. I don't know what frightened him, but I do know he slept with a revolver at his side, and he insisted on going round and locking the doors and windows himself. He became a bundle of nerves, and I couldn't stand it any longer. We had a quarrel, and I left him."

"Yes," said Mike, and his voice was expressionless.

"I wished I hadn't afterwards. He was in a bad way, and it seemed a beastly time to let him down. So I went to the hotel last night." She looked up, and her face was very white, while it was easy to imagine that it was horror that was reflected in her eyes. "I knew his room, and I went straight there. The door wasn't locked, and I went in." She shivered suddenly. "He was lying on the bed. I expect you've seen him."

Mike was silent for a moment, and his hand closed over hers.

"I've heard about it," he said. "What did you do?"

"I came away at once."

"Did you see anyone there?"

"No—only a waiter. He didn't see me." She leaned back against his shoulder, and her eyes were closed. It might have been the shadows which made her look so tired and drawn. "You may as well know it all," she went on. Her right hand sought his, and tightened about it. "Golt came to me a month ago. He wanted information from Arkeld, and he thought I could get it. I promised I'd do what I could, but though Arkeld talked a lot, he didn't give any information away."

Her voice faded, and after a pause Mike said:

134

"Yes?"

"Golt kept worrying me. I had to keep him off, I even made up one or two stories for him. Then there was the quarrel with Arkeld, and—well, I knew Golt had some reason for doing him harm. I believe that Golt killed him. I didn't know what to think this morning, but I knew you were at the Cherry, and I had an appointment there with Golt. I arrived early, and arranged this meeting—I wanted to see you to tell you the truth."

"*Is* it the truth?" Mike asked gently.

She nodded. "I can't prove it."

He noticed that she was shivering a little.

"What is it?"

"It's a queer thing to know when one's going to die," she said.

She uttered the words quietly. They had a strange, disturbing effect on Mike Errol. Either her acting was superb, or she meant it. How was it possible for him to decide which was the truth?

"Who told you that?" he said.

"I know it. Golt doesn't trust me. I gathered that this morning. I'm to be classified as dangerous—oh, I know he's implicated in spying, and I should have strung along with him, but there it is. And you'll get the proof of what I've told you when I'm dead."

He said: "Do you intend to give up living as easily as that?"

She dropped on her knees in front of the fire. The gentle yellow light spread an aura about her, lending an ethereal touch to her loveliness.

"I havn't any choice," she said. "They'll make sure of that. I meant to tell you all I could, that's why I sent for you. Now if you're wise you'll go away."

15
NIGHT OF DISASTER

I t was very quiet in the room.

The rise and fall of their breathing was the only sound, and that was barely audible.

He wanted to believe her.

He wished she would turn so that he could see her face, but something within him stopped him from speaking. When at last she moved it was quickly. She leapt to her feet in a single, graceful movement.

"What tragedy!" she said. "One can't stay on such a level for long. I'm going to make some tea."

He stretched out a hand and took hers.

"Are you sure Golt's as dangerous as you make out?"

"I'm quite sure."

"Why?"

"I had a servant—a little man we called Skippy. I was in a circus once, and he did a turn with an absurd deep voice. It was he who followed you, and told me all that I know about you. You stopped him getting away, and Golt learned of it. I heard Golt giving instructions for him to be released or killed

—it didn't matter which. You see? Skippy was dangerous if he remained in your hands, and I'm dangerous now that I know Arkeld was murdered. There isn't any argument about it. I wish I could think that what I've told you would keep you away from Golt, but that's up to you."

Mike let her go.

He leaned back on the settee, pleasantly aware of the fire's warmth. He longed to believe her and yet there was doubt at the back of his mind.

When she returned, her mood had changed. Gay and brittle, she poured tea and offered small, inconsequential cakes.

Presently Mike put his cup down abruptly.

"Golt isn't all-powerful. Come away with me, and I'll look after you."

"And drag you deeper into it?"

"That's nonsense, I can't get any deeper."

She shook her head. "No, whatever it is, I'll take it. I've told you all I can. I know that Golt has some way of contacting Berlin, though I don't know how he does it. What will you do about him?"

"I'm not the boss," said Errol.

She said wearily: "Well—I think it's time you went. I'm seeing Golt at the Cherry Club again tonight, and I don't think anything will happen until after that. It was—brave of you to come alone," she added. "Do you mind going now?"

Still torn by doubts, he left her, glad of the cooler, clearer air of the streets. He hesitated for some minutes by his car, then drove to the nearest telephone callbox. There he put a call through to Craigie.

"I'd have Myra Berne watched closely, Gordon."

"That's looked after," said Craigie. "What luck did you have?"

137

"I'm coming over now," said Mike, "but I thought I'd better lose no time about getting the girl watched."

Craigie said:

"Go and see Loftus—I shall be out in a few minutes time. Give him the report, Mike."

Mike replaced the receiver then re-entered his car. He drove blindly without thought or aim for about fifteen minutes, regaining a little of the impersonal calm so necessarily a part of an agent's outlook. He did not know that his cousin had seen him enter and leave Byng Mansions, nor that two other Department men were also watching the flat.

They did not see Myra Berne come out.

Nor did they see anyone go in. In fact the watchers were prepared to swear that no one went into Number 32, nor came out. The first intimation of trouble came with the explosion. It rocked the walls of the flat in which an agent was waiting, hurling pictures and furniture crashing to the floor. It was virtually the same as the explosion which had so startled the conference and the Landon Hotel.

It was, however, more effective.

It came from Flat 32, and after the explosion there was a fire which made it impossible for anyone to get in, and which forced a state of emergency on the immediate neighbourhood. The other flats were hurriedly cleared, fire-engines came with their emergency crews, cordons were flung around the blocks, and for two hours the fire raged. By eight o'clock the worst was over, and a few of the tenants were able to return.

No one had entered Flat 32. Nothing was left of it—or of the beautiful woman known to Mike Errol as Myra Berne.

Golt did not visit the Cherry Club that evening.

Golt, in fact, had completely disappeared.

It was his own fault, Loftus told Craigie bitterly. A more careful watch should have been kept, but Loftus had been sure that for the time being Golt felt himself safe, and had advised giving the man enough rope to get himself nicely entangled. It was a trick which had served often enough in the past, but this time it had failed. The flat was deserted, but there were signs of hurried packing—so hurried that some things had been forgotten.

Beneath floor-boards were found three portable transmitting and receiving sets of the type used by spies and discovered too frequently up and down the country. There was nothing else, except that fact that the sets were German made, and left little doubt of Golt's major activity—nor, as Mike Errol said, of the truth of Myra's story.

Over Loftus's flat there was a pall of depression.

The débâcle had come with such devastating suddenness. Loftus had not believed it possible that Golt would clear out so abruptly.

Loftus said, as if to himself:

"I warned him, deliberately, and I didn't watch him. I let the swine slip through without any trouble, and . . ." his face was pale and gaunt as he broke off, and none of the others said a word. There was nothing to say—they had made a complete failure of a job which had once appeared to be going so smoothly. They saw no consolation in the fact that there remained lines of inquiry to be followed up. The disappearance of Golt and the explosion and fire at Byng Court seemed to cut the ground from under their feet.

There was worse to come.

The Prime Minister, irritated if not angered by Mortimer's request for an inquiry, had called for a full report to satisfy the Director-General. Craigie made the report in person, and he was still at 10 Downing Street.

Moreover, Fortescue had disappeared.

The S.B. man watching him had also been lost. It was a matter only of a few hours, but the north-countryman had had an important dinner appointment, and he had not kept it. It was nearly half-past nine when Miller rang through, with the brief report that Fortecue's shadow had been found dead on the Great West Road, the apparent victim of a car crash.

Loftus took the message, thanked Miller, and replaced the receiver.

"It needed just that," he said, staring moodily before him. He told them what had happened, and again there was silence until Thornton said:

"Damn it, Bill, there are things left."

"Tell me what," said Loftus glumly. "Martin Best is checking up on Arkeld's secretary, I know. Farrow's record has been traced—he *is* a waiter, he has been one all his life. *La Reine* hasn't seen Golt for five years—every Theatre Manager in London swears to it—even when she's seen him at theatres she's cut him. I've been playing with high-flown theories and not doing the work I should do. I've been setting Mortimer against the others, I've been creating a fine series of complications, while leaving the eseential jobs to look after themselves."

"Damn it, it can't be as bad as that," said Mark Errol.

"It not only can be, it *is*," said Loftus sharply.

It was rare that there was anything approaching discord amongst the Department agents, and Mark tightened his lips and refused to make the sharp retort that would have been excusable.

After another period of gloomy silence Loftus's face began to clear and he gave a tentative smile. Immediately the atmosphere lightened. None of them had seen him in a mood of such complete dejection before; it had worried them more than they liked to admit.

"Sorry, Mark," he said briefly. "Actually we're so short-handed that we had to take some chances, and we took the wrong ones. There *is* an angle which we haven't followed. It came to me a few minutes ago, but it's not for airing until I've brooded over it pretty thoroughly. Gentlemen, I would be alone."

It was a fine night, free from raids.

That unusual combination was not explained to the public, and in fact there was no official reason for the failure of the raiders to visit Great Britain. Yet there were people who did not think it was entirely a coincidence, when the morning arrived and the full truth was learned.

It had been a night of disaster.

First the news had come in from several areas on the South-Western region of fires and explosions at food depots. They had been on a scale similar to that in the thirty-ninth area, but were more widespread. By three o'clock, word was received of similar sabotage in the North and the Scottish regions. The methods of destruction varied—sometimes by flood, sometimes fire, sometimes explosion. There was of course some connection amongst them, but it was impossible to trace it. Not once during the night was anyone seen acting suspiciously. Not in one case amongst fifty-seven grievous acts of sabotage was there the slightest indication of how it had been contrived, or by whom.

It was as if nature had made a freak decision, and had acted on its own.

That, of course, was nonsense.

Loftus knew it when he was awakened at five o'clock by a

call from Craigie, and was told to go at once to Number 10. Hershall knew it, when Mortimer presented him—a little before that phone call—with the full facts. It had been a diabolical contrivance to make each disaster—and they amounted to disasters—happen at the same time. There was no way of explaining them except by carefully planned sabotage on a scale which was frightening. More damage to food was done in that one night than by six months of German bombing. It was difficult to make a full estimate, but Sir Bruce Mortimer, pale and tight-lipped told Hershall, Craigie, Loftus and three other members of the War Cabinet that a food supply reckoned to last the region for two weeks had been destroyed in six hours.

Hershall took it as might have been expected—with a nod and a frown, and a few moments of concentration. Then he looked up at Craigie.

"You've got no information for me?"

"No," said Craigie briefly.

"Nothing has come of your inquiries?"

"Nothing beyond the earlier report," said Craigie.

"I see. Loftus . . ." the shrewd eyes were turned towards the big man. "You haven't failed us like this before."

"I hope I haven't failed you yet, sir," said Loftus.

"Can you expect a further demonstration of inability to cope with a crisis?" snapped Mortimer. "I believed when I saw you this morning that there was some reason to think you had made progress towards the solution of a problem that was not then serious but only threatened to become so. Now . . ."

"Yes, yes," said Hershall, cutting sharply through the verbosity of the Director-General. "What have you in mind, Loftus?"

"It's not in the form of a report, sir."

"I don't want a report, I want your ideas."

"If I may be permitted to interrupt," said Mortimer icily. "Mr. Loftus inferred this morning that the trouble was caused by reactionaries, probably Communist, working in the depots and warehouses. Since then I have been able to get a full report on Communist activities, and there is no evidence in support of this theory."

Loftus said evenly: "I was talking to six strangers. Sir Bruce, and I saw no reason to confide in them."

"They were six fully accredited . . ."

"We really haven't time for acrimony," said Hershall sharply. "What do you think, Loftus?"

Loftus said: "Briefly, that Arkeld was murdered, and the explosion was staged at the Landon to give each member of the conference reason to be aware of personal danger."

"The earlier belief was that the explosion misfired." said Hershall. "You don't think it was intended to kill them?"

"I didn't at the time," said Loftus. "Here is a thing carefully planned and executed. It has been going on for months. Arkeld was killed the moment there was some reason to believe that the leakage which affected his area was discovered. I stress the world *leakage*, gentlemen. Men who are afraid will do things which normally they would not consider."

"I don't follow you," said the Minister of Supply.

"Go on," said Hershall keenly.

"This way, sir," said Loftus. "The most important men in the Food Ministry, outside the Minister, are Sir Bruce and the regional directors. They have a comprehensive knowledge of the arrangements in their districts, and they can put their hands on the detailed storage and transfer arrangements at any moment. If any one of them could be frightened sufficiently to pass on that information, the receiver of it would destroy a whole area—one sixth of the country's food reserve."

He paused, and looked away from Hershall, conscious of Mortimer's impressed, certainly startled stare.

Hershall said calmly:

"I see. It's interesting. But could any one of the gentlemen be so easily frightened?"

"From my knowledge of them it is impossible," said Mortimer slowly. "They would resign rather than do it."

"I don't know," said Loftus. "The threat of death is a pretty potent weapon—certain death, that is, like Arkeld's. It would take more than ordinary courage to resist. And there is one thing that has perhaps been overlooked. We know of the events of the past two days—but do we know whether any of the regional directors have been subjected to a long period of personal menace?"

"I don't believe that any of them would have dealings with our enemy in any circumstances," and Mortimer sharply.

Loftus shrugged: "I've merely submitted a possibility, and one which I think should be followed up," he said. He looked into the Prime Minister's eyes, and Hershall returned the stare. "It means a complete check on the activities of all the regional directors during the past year, sir, and I think it can only be done by asking their cooperation."

Mortimer exclaimed: "That's impossible!"

Hershall looked round at him.

"Nothing's impossible, Mortimer," he said mildly. "I think Loftus is right. What exactly do you want to do?"

"Ask each one whether he has received direct or indirect threats. There's no time to lose, sir." Loftus smiled a little, and then turned a bland and gentle stare on Sir Bruce Mortimer. "Have you been threatened, Sir Bruce?" he asked mildly, and when he finished every eye turned towards the Director-General, and for a while there was silence.

It grew strained the longer it remained unbroken.

16

EFFECTS OF FEAR

The first movement after Loftus's question was from Hershall, who took his cheroot case from his pocket and deliberately chose one. It happened that the Minister of Supply and the other War Cabinet members were on one side of the room, behind Loftus or at least out of his sight, and only Mortimer, Hershall and Craigie were clear in his line of vision. He watched the Director-General closely. It was possible that the man was merely showing his displeasure, and that he would rap out a crisp disclaimer when he had waited long enough.

The Prime Minister might have been expected to get impatient, for it was not yet six o'clock in the morning, and he had been roused an hour before. He did not; Loftus had come to believe that Hershall was a man who always did exactly the right thing.

When he broke the silence it was mildly:

"Would you rather think it over, Mortimer?"

That worked, for the Director-General's fixed, glassy stare broke, and he sat back a little in his chair.

"It has been an extremely worrying time," he said. "Extremely worrying. Loftus's suggestion has taken me very much by surprise. However, I know that I can rely on anything I said being treated in full confidence."

"Of course," said Hershall.

"Thank you. You may know that I am a collector of emeralds—I might say that the hobby was the most important thing in my life until I was given the opportunity of serving my country." He spoke a little stiffly, as if to play down all sentiment. "In the collecting of precious stones one comes across strange people and strange things. About a year ago the famous Keltov Emeralds were on the market, and I bought them—at what was, I will admit, a ridiculously low price. Before I did so, I was telephoned and told that I would pay at least double that amount I offered, or that I would lose my life." Mortimer spoke in a dry voice which gave the story a strange dramatic quality. "I have been threatened before—any collector will tell you that when family heirlooms change hands, cranks in the family will say and do absurd things."

Loftus broke in quietly: "May I suggest something else?"

"What is it?" asked Mortimer.

"You had advanced a certain sum on these stones, and bought them in when interest was not maintained?"

Mortimer swallowed an invisible lump in his throat.

"That is so. It was a business matter and I dealt with it as such. But from that time onwards I was constantly harried, by telephone and by letter. It was not a matter which I wished to pass on to Scotland Yard, but I will admit that I was worried. I— I had an idea of the actual complainant," he went on, and there was perspiration on his forehead. "That was why I did not hand the matter over to the authorities. Understand that nothing has actually been done, but—it has made it necessary to live in a constant atmosphere of tension. I lost myself only when I was immersed in my work, but the matter came to a head about a week ago."

They waited when he paused, and there was a general exclamation when he said:

"I sent the Keltov Emeralds back to their original owner, without any request for a return of the loan. I did not mention it. I believed that I would then be free of complications, and could apply myself fully to my work. I was worried by the trouble with Arkeld, you understand. But—the threats continued."

He broke off abruptly. Hershall looked at him, and his expression was both thoughtful and understanding.

"That was a nasty experience, Mortimer. We won't ask you now to substantiate the facts, of course, I know that they're quite true. You've no objection to Mr. Loftus asking questions?"

"Naturally not.'

"The only questions I need to ask can be put later," smiled Loftus, "and in the meantime Sir Bruce might care to draft out the essential factors—the names of the people concerned, and of all who may have known of the transaction. There is just one thing—were any demands made on you after you returned the emeralds?"

"No," said Mortimer. "There were threats—vague and yet disturbing. It—it was suggested that I should retire from the Ministry. Of course, I should have reported this in due course, but I did not realise until tonight that it could be in any way connected with the graver issues."

"Of course not." Hershall was still soothing. "And you'll do that draft?"

"Yes, immediately."

"That's good," said Hershall. "Let me know what happens as soon as you can, Loftus."

Loftus and Craigie were the first to leave Number 10. The dawn was already showing grey in the skies, and a surprising number of people were about. The usual police and military guard over the Prime Minister's house was there, of course, grim figures in the raw light.

Craigie and Loftus walked to the Department office. As they went Craigie asked quietly:

"What gave you that idea, Bill?"

"It was a combination of pointers," said Loftus slowly. "I first had a feeling when I was at the conference that they were all on edge. I wondered why, although I put it down to the death of Arkeld and the explosion. But a talk with Miller made it clear that the explosion could not have done any serious harm to anyone in the conference room, and had that been intended it could have been contrived. You follow?"

"Yes, go on."

"Well, it looked as if someone was trying to throw a scare into them. And Arkeld's death could have been intended for the same thing. I spent some hours trying to work it out last night, and came finally to the conclusion that if the regional directors or area commissioners were *frightened* of something they might be more easily persuaded to talk. Not all of them, but some of them. And there's a skeleton in every cupboard," he added more lightly. "Our job is to find out what it is. We can't go slowly, now—direct approach is the only thing that matters. I've been looking through the general reports you've given me," he added as they reached the entrance to the building. "There are duplicate records in twenty places of the location of storage dumps for food—*but the records are in every case complete.* Golt—if our man is Golt—needs to find only one of those duplicates, and he knows the exact position of all our emergency supplies. If he can get one of the directors in a frame of mind to give him a duplicate—well, there you are."

148

Craigie said quietly; "Let's get upstairs."

They went up in silence, and sat in easy chairs. The fire had burned low, but this time Craigie did nothing to mend it. He looked old and very grey as he fingered a meerschaum, but he did not take out his tobacco pouch.

"Two things, Bill. Do you think our man could be other than Golt?"

"Yes," said Loftus.

"Why?"

"It's early to say, and it will take time," said Loftus. "What's the other thing?"

"We have assumed up to now that the sole aim of all this intimidation is to get hold of a duplicate. But surely the events of the night suggest that he already *has* one!"

Loftus said: "I'm afraid he has."

"Then he can use it for similar sabotage all over the country."

"If we don't stop him," said Loftus quietly. "Gordon, I'm being annoying, I know, and making more mystery than there is, but if I started talking now I'd be at it all day. The whole affair is a series of vague shapes in my mind, and I think they'll make a pattern before long, but not just yet. All right?"

Craigie smiled. "Yes, I won't worry you. What are you going to do now?" he broke off, for Loftus lifted the telephone.

"Call the others."

He telephoned Carruthers, and told him to tell the Errols and Thornton to go to the Landon Hotel. That done he looked at Craigie.

"Are you coming?"

"Send for me if you want me," said Craigie. "I must get the details of the night's work co-ordinated. They aren't going to be good," he added with a grimace.

Loftus smiled and nodded and went out.

JOHN CREASEY

As he drove to the Landon his thoughts were not of Hershall or of the Area Commissioners. They were of Craigie, and the fact that Craigie was tired. It was not so much a physical tiredness as a mental lassitude. It was obvious to Loftus that Craigie would have to take a spell of rest in the next few weeks, or he would crack. He thought that Craigie realised it, but fought against it.

Loftus did not know of a single week in the past ten years when Craigie had been free from some affair or other. Loftus drew up at the Landon.

In five minutes Carruthers had joined him, and in another ten, the Errols. Spats Thornton arrived almost on their heels. The reception clerk put a room at their disposal, and on their way to it they saw that workmen were busy putting right the walls which had been damaged by the explosion.

Once in the room, Loftus spoke quickly and to the point. Thornton was to be with him: the Errols and Carruthers were to be at the three ways of approach to the first floor passage off which the bedrooms opened. That settled, Loftus and Thornton gave the others time to get to their places, and then made their own way to the suite where Lord Brelling was sleeping.

He tapped on the door, and a valet opened it. Loftus showed his card. The man protested that his Lordship was asleep, but Brelling raised no objection when he was awakened. He looked tired but he was affable enough as he nodded to them.

"Well, what's it all about?"

Loftus told him of the night's disasters. Brelling's smile disappeared, and so did his sleepiness. He made little comment, but was swearing lustily when Loftus finished.

"The Department is doing its best," Loftus assured him. "A theory has been advanced that the organiser of the sabotage is using a simple weapon for getting information—fear, in short. We've got to find him. We think you can help us."

"What do you think I'm afraid of?" demanded Brelling.

"I don't know," said Loftus, and then gently: "I didn't even suggest the weapon was being used against you."

Brelling stretched his hands for cigarettes.

"I'm not scared, Loftus, but you're a clever devil. I've had a lot of trouble with threatening letters and telephone calls. Had 'em ever since I can remember. My method is to put 'em in the waste paper basket and ignore 'em. There was a time when I went to the police, but I gave that up."

"Have they grown more insistent?"

"The last I had demanded that I should retire—or be killed," Brelling said drily.

"A letter or a phone call?"

"A phone call."

"Have you any idea who sent it?"

"No," said Brelling, "but the voice was very deep—I could hardly understand the words at first. I—what's the matter, Loftus? You look startled."

"Startled is one word," said Loftus. "Satisfied is another. It gives us some help, and we want it badly. You've no idea at all, you say, who might be threatening you?"

"Not the faintest."

"What has been the excuse?"

Brelling shrugged. "That I make too much money. Disgruntled shareholders and these people and that—you don't need telling they exist, I suppose?"

"No," said Loftus. "But if you can I'd like a summary of the numbers of threats and anything interesting about them, during the past three months. Will you prepare that for me?"

Brelling nodded. "All right. I suppose you know you've ruined my night's rest," he added good-humouredly.

"Quite a hearty," murmured Thornton, as they left the apartment. "Do you believe he's quite as disinterested as he appears to be?"

"We'll find out," said Loftus.

He was surprised to find that Sir Augustus Gray was up and fully dressed. The south-eastern director was in riding-clothes, and he looked surprised when he saw Loftus and Thornton—and a little annoyed.

"Well, what's all this about?" He was abrupt.

Loftus told him, going through the same routine as with Brelling, Gray had been standing for the beginning of the story, but slowly he backed to a chair, and sat down. He looked more worried than Brelling had done—in fact he looked a man for whom nothing could make up for the disasters of the night.

Loftus said: "And it is obvious that one of the duplicate reports has got into the wrong hands. It isn't a thing that could be stolen easily, but it could have been given."

"Don't talk out of the back of your head," snapped Gray, but there was no sting in his voice. He hesitated for some seconds, and then continued jerkily:

"I have been approached for a copy, Loftus. A private matter has been causing me some trouble—in short, blackmail. I'm not going to beat about the bush. A woman. Letters." He stood up and tapped his riding-crop against his breeches. "I was offered them for a copy."

"Yes?"

"Turned it down, of course," said Gray. "Disturbing, all the same. I didn't want the matter to become public, but if it must it must. I've heard nothing since."

"When was this?"

"A week ago."

"Was it telephoned?"

"Yes, by a man with a remarkably deep voice."

"Ah," said Loftus. "Well, all being well the gentleman won't trouble you again."

Gray brushed a hand over his thinning hair.

"I won't go out," he said. "I'll be here if I'm wanted."

Loftus thanked him, and went to Sanderson's room. Sanderson was asleep, but showed no annoyance at being awakened. He heard Loftus out gravely, and then began to collect his shaving gear.

"I must get up," he said. "This is bad, Loftus."

Loftus went through the routine, but with Sanderson he drew a blank, even with direct questioning. The mellow voice was a trifle harsh as he answered "no" to various questions, demanding to know what Loftus was getting at.

Evading the question, Loftus went along to Whittaker's suite. He had left the Scottish regional director until last because he expected more difficulty from him than from any of the others. In this he was right, for the difficulty started early. There was no reply to his knock, nor any response when the telephone operator rang his bedside telephone.

The door was locked.

Loftus sent for the floor waiter. It was Farrow, who showed no surprise or recognition, but obediently tried his his master-key. The lock turned, but the door was bolted.

"We'll have to have it down," said Loftus quietly.

He sounded worried, and Thornton knew that he was afraid that some harm had come to Whittaker. A quick trip to the Errols and Carruthers brought the assurance that no one had passed in or out of the area, and Loftus returned to Whittaker's door. He needed only to exert his full weight once before the door went in, and he stumbled forward into the room.

It was empty, but the bedroom door was ajar.

Loftus stepped through, finding it difficult to control his fears, and with a vision of Arkeld's face clear in his mind's eye. But he did not find Whittaker dead.

He did not find him unconscious.

And worse; the Scottish regional director was stripped to the waist, and his wrists were fastened to the head-panel of the bed. His head was lolling on to his chest, and it was his chest which made Loftus tighten his lips, and brought an exclamation from Thornton, for it was burned in a dozen places, and the ugly, reddish-browned marks of the burns were fresh.

Loftus went forward quickly, and raised the man's head. He was not surprised to find a gag in his mouth, and he took that out gently, while Thornton telephoned for a doctor, a Dr. Little, who had often done confidential work for the Department. Between them they unfastened Whittaker's thin, bony arms, and rested him on the bed so that his body relaxed.

He showed no signs of returning consciousness.

They searched the room, but they found nothing, although they even looked in drawers and in small cupboards, for there was the possibility that the dwarf and Topsy had been concerned in this. The bathroom window was open, however, and it led to a fire-escape. It seemed to Loftus that the torture had stopped at his knocking, that the devils who had done this thing had made good a quick escape. The exits were watched, of course, but the perpetrators might well have done no more than go to another room in the hotel, *via* the fire-escape. Loftus telephoned instructions to the police on duty to have the doors watched and to allow no one, staff or residents, to go out. It was early enough for that to cause no great inconvenience, although if a room-by-room search became necessary Leroux would not be pleased.

Much depended on whether Whittaker could talk when he

came round. He had been knocked out by a blow on the back of the head and so savagely that it might have caused concussion. There was nothing to do but wait for Dr. Little—or so it seemed, before the telephone rang.

Loftus lifted the receiver, and he had a shock—one that he thought was as great as any he had received in that affair. For the words that came immediately were so deep that he could hardly understand them, and not until the speaker had finished and closed down did he understand just what they were.

The Shrimp, known—according to Myra Berne—as Skippy, was dead, but his surely inimitable voice had said:

"Put him right out and get away quick."

That was all.

17
"TO THE PUBLIC"

L oftus recovered from the shock of hearing the voice quickly. Of the Shrimp's death there was no conceivable doubt, but of the resurrection of his voice there was all the evidence that was needed. A trick of impersonation of course— possibly a dozen circus performers in the country could do it. Loftus considered the actual facts of the situation.

Whittaker tortured: he had never expected to feel sorry for that fish-like gentleman, but he did so now. Moreover the number of burns proved that whatever his torturers had wanted to get from him had not been forthcoming; the man had physical courage to the highest degree.

That was one thing.

Another, and perhaps of less importance, was the fact that the man with the deep voice had telephoned the brief instructions. *"Put him right out and get away quick."*

"Right out" clearly meant "kill him." It was obvious that whoever had telephoned had known that trouble was developing at the Landon Hotel. As clearly the hotel was being

SABOTAGE

watched, and the warning had been sent because it was known
that Whittaker was likely to be visited.

There was a puzzling thing there.

Loftus and the others had been in the hotel for at least
half-an-hour. The watchers must have seen him enter, and yet
had left it as long as this to telephone him. A vagrant idea that
they had waited until he was actually at the door of Whittaker's suite faded quickly. Even had they been close at hand and
able to do that, they would not have waited until the door was
broken down, and five minutes had elapsed with them in the
room.

The inference was, then, that someone else who could be
dangerous had just entered or was about to enter: someone
who would go to visit Whittaker.

Loftus moved over to the telephone. Thornton eyed him
expectantly. The big man gave the impression that he had
discovered something of importance.

He spoke to the Special Branch O.C.

"No one has left the hotel, or tried to?"

"No, sir, not for at least ten minutes before you telephoned
me to get the doors closed."

"Good. Has anyone come in?"

"One or two people, yes." The man seemed worried. "You
said nothing about people entering, did you?"

"No," said Loftus. "Who are they?"

"I don't know them, but I can find out from the desk clerk.
They've just started upstairs . . ."

"By the stairs?"

"Yes."

Loftus closed down with only a murmured "thanks" and
stepped quickly to the door. He beckoned Spats.

"Two people are coming here, Spats—almost certainly to

this floor, as they haven't troubled to take the lift. Tell the others to close in."

"Right." Thornton went out quickly.

Loftus was left alone in the room, with only a door between him and Whittaker. It flashed through his mind that whoever was coming might be the doctor, but he dismissed that idea; there had been no time. Possibly they were innocent enough hotel residents who had been out during the night, or even for an early morning walk, but most likely one or the other of them had inspired that belated message from the man with the deep voice.

A moment later the door opened, and Thornton poked his nose through. He regarded Loftus with a somewhat pitying air.

"It's definitely not your good day, Bill."

"Why?" Loftus almost snapped the word.

"It's Craigie, and Mortimer's with him."

Loftus stared for a moment in acute disappointment. And then he reasoned that Craigie and Mortimer together would naturally inspire the warning to get away, and he saw the funny side of it. He greeted them quickly, adding:

"I'd hoped you were two badly wanted men, things looked that way." The humour died from his face. "For the rest, it's not at all funny," he said, and he told them what had happened to Whittaker. Mortimer stood tight-lipped on the threshold. He had not had much colour when he had entered; he had none when he turned away. Loftus hardly knew whether to be glad or sorry that Doc Little, a large fat man who regularly overflowed any chair that he sat in, came in soft-footed and, after a few minutes, pronounced an *interim* judgment.

"He won't be long in coming round," he said. "Nothing to worry about there. The blow on the head might leave an effect of mild concussion, but it isn't likely."

"Is he a hospital case?" asked Loftus.

"Oh, no. A nurse will see him through all right." Little was a comforting man, and at no time had Loftus known him more comforting than he was then.

"Wouldn't it be better for him to be somewhere quieter?" Loftus asked, and Little agreed—not because it was medically important, but because he believed that Loftus wanted Whittaker away from the Landon. A nurse arrived, an ambulance was summoned, and Whittaker was taken out of the back door of the Landon.

Craigie had gone to Mortimer's suite, and when Loftus joined them he found Brelling and Gray there. Sanderson had not, apparently, heard of Mortimer's arrival. Loftus was conscious of a restraint in the room when he entered, and he did not need two guesses to know what it was.

Gray, Mortimer and Brelling all had admitted to a skeleton in the cupboard. None would want the others to know of it: all realised that Loftus could betray the confidences if he wished to. His mind took him back to the conference, when he had first seen these men together, and he remembered clearly that a similar restraint had been evident then. It was explained now; they were men who were being systematically frightened, and the job was being done well.

Threats by letter and by telephone, the cunning discovery of each man's secret, or at least an episode in their lives they would not want made public. The gradual playing on their nerves, and then the hints of their resignations, Arkeld's violent death, the explosion, and now Whittaker.

He wondered whether Mortimer had told the others about Whittaker, and as if reading his thoughts the Director-General said:

"We have been discussing the matter, Loftus, and I have put forward your view that some of these things have been done to—er—frighten us. We agree that poor Whittaker's experience is just such a trick. It is a relief to feel that we know what we are facing."

"Ye-es," said Loftus. "And when Whittaker comes round he may be able to tell us something of his attacker. I think he, or they, might well be in the hotel. No one should go out until Whittaker has been able to look the residents and the staff over."

It was Brelling who spoke first in answer.

"My God!" he said, "that will cause a flurry! Is it necessary, Loftus? We don't want to attract a lot of publicity, you know, and we're pretty close to the bone as it is."

Loftus looked keenly at the peer, wondered what was going on behind those heavy-lidded eyes.

"The situation as I see it is just this. Someone is in a position to do the damage that was done up and down the country last night, and he must be found. We can only find him by tracing him through his operatives. Some of those operatives attacked and tortured Whittaker. They may still be in the hotel."

Mortimer said slowly:

"You're right, of course. But it may be a long time before Whittaker is able to identify anyone."

"And he might not be able to then," said Gray unexpectedly. "The men might have been disguised, or masked—damn it, there's melodrama enough in this business already, I don't see why there shouldn't be a bit more."

Loftus shrugged. "Melodrama is a word that has already been suggested by—a Miss Myra Berne." He uttered the name casually but he was looking for reaction. He found none. If facial expression was anything to go by, none of the men in the room had heard it before.

Sanderson's good-humoured face appeared at the door then, but beneath the good humour Loftus imagined there was a degree of nervousness not altogether easy to explain. Sanderson, if he had told the truth, was the one man without a skeleton in his cupboard. Was that a reason for thinking that he had lied?

Loftus thought on what he knew of the man. A happy domestic life, a pretty wife, three children, his "sporting-pensioners" and his general popularity. He was certainly the best known of the five, and there was at least some reason for thinking that his life held no grounds for blackmail, or threats.

Loftus left it to Mortimer to tell him what had happened, and with Craigie left the room.

"We'll need a special order from the Home Secretary for this job," Loftus said, "and it's not going to be pleasant to get it out of him at this time in the morning."

They hurried down the stairs, and when they reached the foyer they found half-a-dozen people gathered about the revolving doors. Two flustered commissionaires and a policeman confronted them. From a side door, Leroux hurried forward.

His expression was a compound of fury and anxiety.

"Mr. Loftus. This is an impossible situation—my guests must be allowed to come and go as they please."

Loftus looked at him coldly.

"There is a state of emergency in the hotel at the moment. You will receive orders from the police and a warrant from the Home Secretary. If you're wise you'll arrange for anyone who must go out to see you at the office, and I'll make arrangements for someone to be with you who can give permission, if advisable."

"But . . ."

"There aren't any buts," said Loftus.

Yet there were; he saw from the temper of the crowd that there would have to be stronger action to keep the residents quiet, and he sent for the Errols and Carruthers. He put them on the doors, with S.B. men, leaving Spats Thornton to watch the first floor, although that was little more than a formality.

Craigie hurried from the hotel to get the necessary instructions from the Home Secretary, and to tell the Yard of the position. A little more than twenty minutes after he had left, Miller arrived, large and reassuring. He parked himself in Leroux's office and prepared to receive any of the residents who had urgent reasons for leaving. Loftus knew that he would not easily be satisfied.

As the morning advanced the manager's office was besieged, and from time to time Miller's cool voice came through the open door. The foyer was filled, the breakfast room was besieged, the lounges were crowded, and there was but one topic of conversation.

Rumour and speculation increased with bad temper, but Miller allowed only four people to go out; all of them were on Government business, and well enough known for him to take the chance. No word came from Doc Little about Whittaker, and none came about Fortescue, who was still missing. Neither of those things worried Loftus, but he was disappointed about one matter.

La Reine made no request to go out, and he learned that she was staying in bed. So was Rannigan. He hardly knew why he had wanted one or the other to make a fuss about the enforced detention, but there it was.

Craigie returned—some hour after the signed order from the Home Secretary—to find Loftus clearly disappointed.

"What were you expecting?" he asked.

"Someone to get out at all costs," said Loftus, "and it hasn't happened. Great Scott, if this goes on Whittaker will really have to look at 'em all!"

Craigie gave a thin-lipped smile.

"No," he said. "I've phoned Little's nursing home, and Whittaker's now conscious and clear-headed. There were three men; he can only tell us that the man who questioned him had a very deep voice, which he used in a whisper. The three wore masks."

"Oh," said Loftus blankly. "Not another deep voice! What did they want from him?"

"He hasn't said—but he's coming here in an hour."

"The man certainly has guts," said Loftus, "and I'm beginning to take to him more than I did. Well, there's one other thing. Mortimer and the others aren't happy. In fact, they're scared—and I can't say I blame them. I've had a chat with each in turn, and I can't get anything more out of them."

"How much longer do you want to keep the hotel sealed up?" asked Craigie.

Loftus considered. "Well, as Whittaker can't do much, we'll have to let things go after lunch. I'd like to hold the situation until half-past two, though."

"You seem quite certain the people are here," said Craigie.

"I am." Loftus rubbed his long chin. "No one got out. That's a fact. They may be circus performers, but they can't do disappearing tricks. I—hallo, what's this?"

In a flurry of footsteps the door burst open to reveal Thornton and Leroux, and both men were carrying leaflets. Thornton thrust one of them into his hand.

It did not make nice reading, and his face hardened as his eyes moved along the lines. Craigie was reading another, his expression equally gaunt.

For they read:

TO THE PUBLIC

There were no raids on this country last night. But there were attacks against which there is and will be no defence. It is estimated that one-twentieth of the WHOLE NATION'S FOOD SUPPLY was destroyed by sabotage in six hours.

The Government has kept this from you—but it will soon have to admit the truth. ENGLAND FACES STARVATION.

That was all.

There was no suggestion of what action should be taken, if any, no kind of ultimatum. It was a bare statement of facts— within limits, for the "one-twentieth" was a considerable exaggeration. The abruptness of it would do one thing only: spread disquiet among the people.

"Where were these found?" Craigie asked quietly.

"In the first corridor," said Thornton. "Mine was, at least."

"Mine was found in the lift," said Leroux.

"About what time?"

They said together: "Ten minutes ago."

"Nice work," said Loftus in a too calm voice. "They're in the hotel all right, Gordon, and the leaflets were printed well ahead of schedule, for distribution if the papers had nothing about the sabotage." He looked at Leroux, who took the hint and went out, promising to say nothing of what he had read. "This is even a worse sabotage than the other," Loftus went on sombrely, "for it aims at destroying public morale."

"Damn it, a few leaflets . . ."

"A few?" asked Loftus bleakly. "I wish it could be."

But it was not; and both he and Craigie had felt when they had first seen the leaflet that they would not be confined to the Landon. It was the Assistant Commissioner at Scotland Yard who telephoned them first, to say that he was getting reports that the leaflet was being found in all parts of the country. It was impossible to estimate the number distributed, but by two o'clock that afternoon it was clear that they ran into hundreds of thousands.

And not once was a distributor found.

The intention behind it was obvious: it was a deliberate and well-judged attempt to spread public disquiet, and it could only be countered by outright denial. The radio programmes were interrupted with that object, special editions of the papers giving a guarded statement of the truth were put on the streets, but outright denial as such was impossible, and Loftus as well as Craigie knew that the effect of the leaflet would be disastrous unless it could be off-set within forty-eight hours.

It was a crisis of the first order, admitted, in fact, by Hershall before the War Cabinet early that afternoon to be the blackest moment of the war.

At three o'clock, while the Landon was still in a state of siege, Loftus said to Craigie:

"I don't believe Golt is the leader, he hasn't the brain for a stunt like this. Someone in the hotel probably knows a lot more about it than Golt ever will. They *must* be here, or the leaflets couldn't have been put around. And they'll have to get away sooner or later, or try to."

Craigie said: "It's more than urgent, Bill."

"Don't I know it! Another night like last night and there'll be a six months step backwards in the war. I . . ."

He broke off suddenly, listened, then stepped to the door and flung it open. A horrifying sound rushed into the room, that of people in fear or in agony—women's voices mingling with men's in shouts and screams. It was some way off, but the background tap-tap-tap-tap was ominously clear to the listeners.

Loftus started for the passage. In the foyer, or somewhere near it, he knew, a machine-gun was being used. He reached the end of the passage, but then he pulled up short, for he saw Farrow standing in front of him; and Leroux the manager at Farrow's side.

Both men held automatics pointing towards him.

18

HOTEL TRAGEDY

I t was as quick as that, and as unexpected.
Loftus heard Craigie come out of the room behind
him. Then he saw Farrow's gun rise a matter of an inch, and
he flung himself forward.

It was the only thing to do.

If he stood where he was he would be shot, and there was
at least a chance of spoiling their aim if he moved. He went
with a queerly detached frame of mind, diving low as he
would in a tackle. He heard the sharp reports of two guns, and
an exclamation from Craigie.

He was helped because he was on a patch of polished
parquet, and he slithered along for a foot or more, and was
able to grasp the ankle of one of the men. He heard a bullet
stab into the floor close to his head, but he tightened his grip
and pulled. He felt the man falling, and he swept out his other
arm, catching the second man about the knees.

A bullet cut through the shoulder of his coat.

He felt a sharp pain, but it was of little moment. He tried to
get up, but where the polish had helped him before it was

against him then, and he slipped. But he saw that Leroux was lying on his back, dazed and without his gun. The danger came from Farrow, who was on one knee and pointing the gun towards him.

Loftus flattened right out.

A bullet went over his head, but he knew that if a second one came he would be finished. He was surprised that it did not come, and more surprised when he saw Farrow stagger, a strained expression on the waiter's face. The gun dropped slowly from his hand, and Farrow hit the floor.

Loftus stood up slowly, and as he did so a voice came along the passage.

"All right, Bill?"

It was Thornton. He had a gun in his hand and his face was grave. Loftus leaned for a moment against the wall.

"Thanks to you, yes. Gordon isn't. Where did you spring from?"

"I was watching the Mortimer crowd, when the shooting started in the foyer. The Errols are holding them up."

"Them?"

"See for yourself. I was trying to get round at the back of them."

"Let's have your gun, and see what you can do for him," said Loftus with a motion towards Craigie. As he took the gun he saw Leroux open his eyes, and he did not wait long to decide what to do with him. He bent down and hit the manager on the back of his neck with the butt of the gun.

"Weapon for you on the floor," Loftus said briefly.

Thornton had already seen the gun which Farrow had dropped, and he pocketed it. Loftus stepped quickly towards the foyer, keeping close to the wall.

He was prepared for a shock, but not on the scale he witnessed. At least a dozen people, dead or injured, lay on either side of the foyer, the doors blocked by the bodies of men.

He saw Mike and Mark Errol standing there, one on each side. He saw Carruthers, also; Carruthers was stretched out, unconscious.

Opposite the doors; and at the entrance of the main lounge, were four or five men—he could not be sure how many, for he could not see them clearly. He did recognise Maximilian Golt, who was on one knee behind a heavy chair. He saw an armed dwarf, also, and another man standing behind a pillar which saved him from the Errols, and in his hand was a tommy-gun. The man was reloading, and Loftus took his chance then. He stepped forward into sight, and fired three times. He hit the tommy-gun merchant in the side of the head, Golt in the shoulder and a third man in the thigh. As they fell, the dwarf turned like lightning, and fired. But he fired too soon for the bullet went wide, and by then Loftus had his other gun out; the dwarf went down.

One remained, a thin-faced man. Loftus did not remember having seen him before; but there was no time for worrying about that. He also had a gun, and for the moment it seemed as if he would beat Loftus to the trigger. For the second time that day someone else came to Loftus's rescue, for a bullet snapped from Mike Errol's gun, and the thin-faced man's automatic dropped.

It happened like that.

It was over almost before it had started, and there had been no measurable time for Loftus. From the moment he had heard the screaming and the shouting and the deadly tapping of the machine-gun to the moment when he saw the last man's gun fall, time seemed to have been crowded into an eternity.

The Errols straightened up and stepped forward.

Some people on either side of the foyer also moved, and a

woman began to shriek, high-pitched piercing screams which began to get on his nerves. But he had not spoken before the doors opened on either side of the foyer to admit uniformed policemen, and quite suddenly Loftus knew that for the moment he had nothing to worry about except Golt and his followers. He spoke crisply, and as if nothing untoward had happened.

"We'll get these four into Leroux's office. The tommy-gun merchant won't be talking again."

As the injured men were moved, Mike and Mark told the story piecemeal. They had been by the front doors when the thin-faced man had tried to force his way out. He had been referred to Miller, who had been about to speak to him when the dwarf had appeared in the doorway, and Miller had been shot in the chest.

"Miller too?" said Loftus grimly.

"It's a marvel any of us are left," Mark said laconically. "The tommy-gun merchant just started to open up, intending to carve a way through. Mike and I had gone to one side to see Miller, and to try to get the dwarf. Police and S.B. men crowded in from outside, and were mown down as they came. People at the sides moved and the little swine turned the gun on them. It was a massacre."

Loftus nodded.

"Mike and I dodged to the cover of the doors," said Mark, "And the others were piled up so high we had protection. Spats squeezed away somewhere . . ."

"I've seen him. He got me here."

"Good work. Carruthers took a packet—but a slight head-wound is the limit, I think."

"Well, that's something," said Loftus.

"So your idea worked," said Mike slowly.

Loftus said: "I half wish it hadn't."

But despite the tragedy of those few minutes at the Landon, when in all eleven people were killed and twenty-three seriously injured, he did not wish that the idea had not worked. He had believed that the attackers of Whittaker were in the hotel, and his belief had been vindicated. For under interrogation, and he was not gentle, Golt, the dwarf and the third gunman admitted that they had "questioned" the regional director, but they did not say what it had been about.

That did not matter; Whittaker would talk.

The fourth man whom Mike Errol had wounded was named Letaxa, and he was officially in London collecting subscriptions for Greek relief funds. He cracked completely under Loftus's questioning. Yes, he had official connections in Greece, and his mission was a genuine one, but he was also working under cover with Golt. They had wanted to get the full details of the food storage in England—he could not say for whom, and Loftus believed him. Golt had also wanted to get that information, and Letaxa believed that he had succeeded in getting at least some of it. He had not known of the questioning of Whittaker, but he did know that the dwarf—named Dak—had shot the thirty-ninth area commissioner in his, Letaxa's, room. The body had been taken to Arkeld's room to create the impression that he had been shot there. Farrow had helped to carry the body in, and Farrow—Loftus realised—had lied deliberately about the time of the shot, and what he had been doing; Arkeld had been killed just before two o'clock.

The hotel had been quickly emptied of residents and guests. As the search begun, various details came to light. It became clear that Leroux and Farrow had been working with Golt for a long time, that other servants were also working with them, and that the members of the circus had stayed at the hotel—without registering—for some time past. Topsy and the very fat man with the grey bowler, however, had not been there, although the deep-voiced Skippy had, from time to time.

The only servants who had waited on them had been the men and women in the confidence of Leroux. It was easy to understand when the full truth was known how easily the explosion had been arranged, and how convenient it had been for the murder of Arkeld and for the torture of Whittaker.

Loftus heard reports from time to time at his flat.

There was a small room there which had been prepared for such emergencies as interrogation of the nature then demanded. It was without windows, and its walls and door were sound-proof. It was rarely used, but Loftus proposed to shrink from nothing that day. He left Golt there for a while, and he was about to go into the man when a car drew up outside.

Thornton, watching from the window, reported that Whittaker had arrived, with Sir Bruce Mortimer.

"We'll see 'em first," said Loftus.

One of the first things they learned from Mortimer was that Craigie was out of danger, and that did a great deal to ease the minds of the Department Z men; Craigie was more than a leader, he was a legend. Loftus lit a cigarette as he digested the news, and regarded the regional director of food conservation for Scotland.

Nothing about Whittaker's face had improved. The cold, fish-like eyes, the long curved nose and small mouth with the receding chin all combined to make a bad impression. There were patches under his eyes, and he looked tired, but otherwise he showed no signs of his ordeal.

Loftus was torn between admiration for, and dislike of, the man.

Mortimer cleared his throat.

"The Prime Minister suggested that we came to you, Loftus—as Craigie is unfortunately unable to work. Er . . ." he broke off and looked at Whittaker, whose sharp and unpleasant voice jarred on Loftus's ears.

"This is the position, Loftus. I have for a long time been victimised by blackmailers. Legally all that I have done in the way of business is irreproachable. There is no room for morals or sentiment in such a sphere. I have enemies, and I have always dealt with them myself. For some time after I took up my present position I was not approached, then I was threatened with many dire penalties—unless I resigned. Naturally I refused. Immediately prior to the convening of this conference, I was asked to hand over a copy of the food distribution and storage plan. I refused to do that also. Last night I was visited, and you know what happened. They wanted the plan. I continued to refuse it. That is all I can tell you."

"Thanks," said Loftus quietly. "It may interest you to know that the men who maltreated you aren't precisely enjoying themselves now."

"That doesn't matter." Whittaker waved a hand impatiently. "What matters is a prevention of another affair like last night's."

"Ye-es. Did they give you the impression that they already had one copy?"

"They did not."

"Yet last night's work suggested that they had," said Loftus. "Do either of you know whether Fortescue was also worried by threats and menaces?"

"He gave no one that impression," said Mortimer.

"He's missing, isn't he?" said Whittaker. "They're probably working on him now."

"It could be," said Loftus. He had not yet told any of the directors that Fortescue had been seen with Golt, although he hardly knew why he kept so silent on that point. "Well, gentlemen, as I see it there is only one thing for you to do—that is to get the locations of the storage dumps changed as quickly as possible."

"It will take a month to change them," said Mortimer. "I have of course made sure that all copies of the plan have been collected—there were twenty, and nineteen are now at Number 10. The one which is missing was one of those which Fortescue had."

Both men rose. They were in a hurry, they said, to get back to Whitehall. Sanderson and Gray were already there, and Loftus gathered that there was some argument now as to whether they should have met at the Landon. Loftus knew one thing; they were quite out of their depth in the new developments. None of them seemed to realise the urgency of finding who had the copy of the distribution plan.

It was more than worrying, it was puzzling. A copy was missing, and had, apparently, been acted on. Yet Whittaker had been tortured to get another. "Why? A thousand times why?" Loftus said, aloud as he returned to the Errols and Spats Thornton.

"Answer me that, and we'll know most of it. Now let's get down to questioning Golt."

But they did not question Maximilian Golt after all.

They found him lying on a single bed which was fitted into the small room. He was unconscious, and at first sight he seemed to be dead, but Doc Little, hurriedly summoned, pronounced him to be suffering from acute morphine poisoning.

"I saw him swallow something at the hotel," Mike said. "Or I thought I did."

Loftus drew a deep breath. He said bitterly:

"It doesn't seem to matter a damn what we do or try, we

lose out by minutes every time. We've got just two possibilities left—the grey-bowler gentleman whom Golt called Barker, and the woman midget, Topsy. Just those two. I . . ."

He stopped suddenly.

He appeared to be staring at Mike Errol, but he was actually seeing an idea, and it was growing apace.

He said slowly:

"Add this up, if you can. They've acted on a copy of the plan, but they want one. They planted wireless sets on Golt, and then he ran to the Landon, where it was obvious our attention would be concentrated. I was telephoned by the deep voiced gent—I thought it was a warning to Whittaker's mob, but in fact it was intended that I should take the message, it *made* me concentrate on the hotel." He paused. "Has a penny dropped anywhere?"

The three shook their heads.

"Oh, but it makes sense," said Loftus excitedly. "Can't you see? We were deliberately encouraged to maintain a close watch on the hotel—the Whittaker business fits in well. *They*—whoever they are—have the plan but wanted to create the impression that they haven't. *They* knew that Golt and Letaxa's sphere of usefulness was over, and so *they* arranged for Golt and Letaxa to be put on the spot. They kept me hunting at the Landon—my God, it's the biggest red-herring I've ever smelt."

Mike said dazedly: "Red-herring?"

"Certainly a red-herring. In other words, a pretty trick to get us on the wrong trail. Even Myra helped—she concentrated our ideas on Golt. I couldn't understand why he had been careless enough to leave those radios where they could be found. *All* the evidence pointed towards Golt as a leading agent of German espionage, and we've believed it. *But actually there isn't a single piece of real evidence to suggest that it's German-inspired."*

Mike said slowly:

"It must be, man! Who else would want to destroy our food supplies?"

Loftus said: "Who said they want to? They've got a copy of this plan, they've worked a little on it, but if they'd wished they could have blown the whole works up by now. I'll give you a thousand-to-one that there's no serious trouble tonight."

"I can't see what you're driving at," said Mark helplessly.

"Work it out," said Loftus. "Who except the Bosche would have all this interest in our food? Who else would like to hold a gun at the Government's head? *Someone who can supply food to replace that which has been lost.*" He paused, and then said again: "Work it out. I'm going to see Hershall."

19

CARTE BLANCHE

There was nothing in Hershall's manner to suggest that he was facing one of the great crises of the war. He was alone in his private room at Number 10, and he was sitting at his desk with the inevitable cheroot sticking out from his lips. Loftus thought he looked a little paler than he had that morning, and perhaps more tired. But his voice had the same mellow, unhurried ring, as he motioned casually to a chair.

"I've been hoping you would come, Loftus."

"Thank you, sir," said Loftus. "I'm afraid it's only with ideas again. In fact what I really want is an absolute *carte blanche* to act as seems necessary."

"It seems to me you've got it," said Hershall drily. "Still, go ahead."

"I've had all the assistance I could hope for," said Loftus with appreciation, "but this—well, sir, if I asked the Home Secretary to sign an order for the detention of, say, Sir Bruce Mortimer, it wouldn't be easy. I might get it, after a delay—and a delay might well prove fatal."

"Is Mortimer involved?" Hershall gave no indication that he would be surprised if that was the case.

"I've no evidence—he could be." Loftus began to talk, and continued to do so for ten minutes. The submission on which his argument rested was that the trouble was not Berlin-inspired, but organised and operated from inside the country, and by inside interests. Hershall heard him out, and then said:

"All right, Loftus—but these leaflets." There were several on his desk. "Who would have any purpose served by their distribution outside of Germany?"

Loftus said: "Anyone who wanted to force the Government's hand, sir."

"In what way?"

"Large orders for different foods, at decontrolled prices."

Hershall sat very still, and the room seemed to be still and silent with him. And then he pushed his chair back, and stood up. He walked to the door and back again, his hands behind him, his head lowered so that his chin was almost on his chest. At last he spoke.

"All right, Loftus. Have your *carte blanche*—I'll sign it now." He sat down at his desk, pulled paper and pen towards him and wrote quickly, in a clear bold hand. He handed the order to Loftus. "That will see you through. Now—have you anyone in mind?"

Loftus shook his head.

"What is your opinion of the reason for the series of black-mail and threats?"

"That it's the biggest red-herring of them all," said Loftus. "It has been deliberately conceived to get our minds off the truth. It has weakened the Food Organisation at the top, and the perpetrators can do what they like with it at the bottom. These fires and explosions—only men actually concerned in the work itself can start them. Only men actually up and down

the country can have distributed these leaflets. I would estimate that at least a thousand men have done that."

"Communist?" snapped Hershall.

"Not necessarily."

"You encouraged Mortimer to think you thought so.
Why?"

"I wanted him and the others to think we were on the
wrong track," said Loftus. "It was obvious that each one of
them *could* be playing an important part in it. It remains
possible—I would even say probable."

"Fortescue?" said Hershall.

"It could be. Someone who has agents up and down the
country at all events—a multiple store-owner could do it easily." He smiled a little. "I could be wrong, of course, but I don't
think so."

"Nor do I," said Hershall briefly. "But act fast, Loftus."

"I don't think the need for speed is quite as great as it
seemed to be," said Loftus. "We're going to have a lull."

And he was right. Nothing happened that night, nor the
following night. True, a close watch was kept on all storage
dumps and warehouses, but nothing suspicious was observed,
and there was a complete and utter silence from the *"they"* he
had talked so much about. No more leaflets were distributed,
but Ministry of Information observers reported that the
leaflets had produced a sense of uneasiness in the country
greater than anything which had been known before.

Loftus and the Errols were not idle: nor was Spats Thornton, nor a very large and untidy man, one Martin Best,
returned from a fruitless quest in Bedford, where he had
discovered that Arkeld's secretary was a blameless little
woman who could throw no light on the mystery. But Arkeld's
part had faded into insignificance against the wider issues
now uncovered.

Craigie, Davidson and Oundle were all out of danger.

Superintendent Miller was not so badly hurt as had at first been feared, and he directed Special Branch work from a private ward in the Westminster Hospital. The Ministry of Information let it be known that he had been wounded, and the tragedy of the Landon was published fully, the story given for general consumption being that a ring of spies had been discovered to operate from the hotel, and when cornered had tried to fight their way out.

At the end of the second day of inactivity, Loftus had a complete dossier of the six men possibly involved. He found little beyond what he had already been told, but he did notice one peculiar thing.

Five of the directors had stores up and down the country; only Fortescue's stores covered a restricted area. But Fortescue continued to be missing, despite a search as widespread and thorough as any instigated by the Yard. Every police-station in the country had a photograph of the north-countryman, of Maximilian Golt, and of Myra Berne.

"What's the idea of the last two?" Mike asked; he was always inclined to be touchy on the subject of the actress.

"We want to find what part of the country they've been frequenting," Loftus assured him. None of them knew what was in his mind, nor how it was working. He told them one other thing: that every known smoker of Alexis cigarettes was being investigated by the police.

It was just after seven o'clock on the third day of inactivity that the front door-bell of the flat rang. Loftus was deep in an easy chair, with a foot on the mantel-shelf. Spats went to the door, and was startled out of his wits to find the Prime Minister there.

"Is Mr. Loftus in?"

Spats stepped back a pace.

"Why yes, come in."

"Thanks." Hershall was wearing a fur-lined coat which he unbuttoned as he entered the lounge. Loftus snatched his foot from the mantel-shelf as Hershall thrust a crumpled slip of paper beneath his nose.

"Read that."

It was written in Hershall's own writing, and said briefly:

"The controlled prices of a variety of foodstuffs are too low. I hope the Government will give full attention to the matter. Increases are advisable in the very near future."

Loftus read it twice, and then looked up at the Prime Minister's frowning face.

"Telephoned, I suppose. The speaker didn't, by any chance, have a very deep voice, did he?"

"He did. Indeed. I spoke to him. Well?"

"It fits," said Loftus. "The method of presentation is exactly the same as the leaflet. No threat, no ultimatum—just a bare statement. This gentleman works on the mind. How long ago?" He might have been talking to Craigie.

"About half-an-hour. I came straight over here." He spoke casually and as if pre-occupied, and Loftus wondered what was going on behind that high forehead. "You were very right," he said. "I'm not surprised. You've no idea at all which one it is?"

"None," said Loftus. "But it isn't Fortescue. I think he's been kidnapped—or killed. They might well arrange for us to find his body. Thinking it would take the suspicion off the others."

"Hmm. Well, I've called a special Cabinet meeting for tonight. There'll be further communications, of course. Let us hope that there isn't going to be a further demonstration of their powers." He stood up, nodded briefly at the others, and started to open the door before Thornton got to it. From the window Loftus watched him walking briskly along the street, with two Special Branch men not far behind him.

"Things are moving," said Loftus slowly. "There's just one thing we want, now—the gang's headquarters. They *must* have been seen in some locality or other." He frowned as he re-read the message, and then the telephone rang.

He lifted it; and he was not surprised to hear a deep voice intone softly: "Loftus?"

Loftus motioned quickly to the others. Mike Errol slipped into the next room, and started to get busy on having the source of the call checked; but he was delayed in getting through to Scotland Yard.

"You've had or you will have a visit from the Prime Minister," said the deep voice. "Forget it. If you are wise enough to do this, satisfactory arrangements will be made with the Government, and the whole matter will be treated as a scare. If you don't . . ."

"Yes," said Loftus, encouragingly. "If I don't. . . ?"

"You hardly need me to remind you of the power of chaos and destruction," the deep voice told him.

"But so illuminating to hear of it from the master himself," suggested Loftus pleasantly.

"There is no room for sentiment in this," said the deep voice, sharply. "Sentiment goes ill with you, in any case."

"You flatter me," said Loftus, "not for the shrewdness or otherwise of your opinion, but for the fact that I have been thought worthy of study." He was anxious to keep the unknown on the wire as long as possible, and to this aim he frantically racked his brains for any rejoinder that might keep the other from ringing off.

"I won't warn you again," the voice said, and it lost a little of its depth. "Don't make any mistake."

"No more mistakes," said Loftus. "I've made enough. Goodbye."

He closed down gently, for he had heard Mike Errol speak for the second time, and he knew that Mike would have had results.

Mike had, but they were not particularly fruitful. By fast work the Yard had located the place from which the deep-voiced man had telephoned—a kiosk in Chiswick. Police were moving towards it, but there was little hope that the man would be found. There was a slight chance that he would be noticed by someone near, and that a description would be available, but even that chance failed.

A few minutes later Miller rang up from the hospital. His voice was both gruff and excited.

"I've got something, Loftus."

"Good," said Loftus. "What is it?"

"The actress woman . . ."

"Yes?" Loftus glanced quickly at Mike Errol, and away again.

"She isn't dead," said Miller flatly. "She was seen today at Guildford—she was involved in a minor car accident, and the policeman who made inquiries recognised her."

"Did he get her?" Loftus almost bellowed.

"No," said Miller, "she got away. But a cordon was flung about the whole area. It's being watched so closely that no one will be able to get outside it. She certainly hadn't time to get more than twenty minutes' journey away. Will you go to Guildford?"

"Will I not!" exclaimed Bill Loftus, and when he replaced the telephone he looked up at the others with shining eyes. "We've got a break," he said. "Mike, prepare for a shock, your sorrowing has been wasted. Your lovely put up a wonderful show, but she's alive, and running."

Mike stared: "But—but, that's not possible!"

"Indeed it is, and yet another red-herring has been dragged across our path. You'd think we'd have learnt by now the smell of fish. Hats, coats, cars and Guildford—if we don't get results tonight we never will!"

It was quiet at Larch House.

It was so quiet that it got on the nerves of Braddon and Pam, although neither of them complained a great deal. For three days and nights they had been alone at the top of the house, in two small rooms which had a communicating door, and a bathroom adjoining.

The food, delivered three times a day by what they had first thought was a child, and had then decided was a midget, was good—and they had been supplied with books and magazines, which, in different circumstances would have made tolerable reading.

It was the uncertainty of it which worried them as much as the actual imprisonment. They could see no reason for it, and they had no idea how it was likely to end. So far at least there had been no violence, except the roughness which the grey-hatted man had treated them with when they had first reached Larch House. But twice he had visited them, and each time the glances he had cast on Pam had not been pleasant. He came again.

It was the evening of the fourth day of their imprisonment. They heard his heavy footsteps, then his hand fumbling with keys. The fear and revulsion in Pam's eyes were overlaid with pleading as she looked across at Jim.

"For God's sake don't annoy him," she muttered. "I don't mind what he does."

Braddon said thickly: "I can't promise. If the brute . . ."

The door opened, and Barker staggered in. His fat face was red and congested, and his eyes were blood-shot; even from the door it was possible to smell the whisky on his breath.

Behind the door was a man they had not seen before. He stayed outside when Barker entered with exaggerated care, closing the door behind him. He was wearing his grey bowler hat, and he tipped it at an angle over his eyes as he staggered towards Pam.

"Hallo, dearie," he said. "Come to cheer you up—soft-hearted, that's me. Cheer you up."

He sat unsteadily on a hard chair which threatened to collapse beneath him, breathing heavily.

"Rather be with me, eh, ducky? We could have a fine time—always did like the look o' you. Don't wanter be cooped up in a li'l room all the time. Open air . . ."

Pam looked at Braddon. He was standing tight-lipped, his hands clenched, but he appeared to understand the chance she was trying to convey to him. If she could get outside there was a hope that she could get free, and send help to him. Barker stretched out a hand and touched her wrist, and she did not draw back.

"Out t'night, eh?" said Barker. "That's a pretty! Ned Barker ain't mean, if you treat him right. Know a nice li'l place—pub. Not far away. Ole short-shins won't know you've been out, will 'e? Tha's right. I'll see you later, yes." He lumbered to the door, shut one eye solemnly in an attempted wink, and went out. As his heavy footsteps died away, they stared at each other in silence.

It was then, although they did not know it, that a car drew

up outside the apparently empty house, and Myra Berne jumped out. She was admitted by Topsy, and as she entered the bare hall she heard Barker's heavy footsteps thumping down the stairs. His hoarse voice was raised in what was doubtless meant to be a song.

"She leerrrves me, she lerves me, hi-ri-tiddley-hi, she lerves me!"

Myra Berne stepped forward very softly and waited for him.

20
QUICK WORK

Barker put each foot forward slowly, and then dropped heavily and deliberately on to the next stair. The wood creaked and the landing window shook a little with each step. His voice grew louder as he drew nearer the hall.

"She lerves me, she lerves me . . ."

"Barker!"

The woman's voice pierced the fat man's bemused mind, and he withdrew a foot sharply. A look of disgust crossed her face as the whisky fumes reached her.

"You drunken swine," she said dispassionately. "What have you been doing to that girl?"

"Cor luv a duck!" exclaimed Barker, and he raised himself to his full height with drunken solemnity. "Gor bless my soul! Drunk? Who's drunk? Me?"

"What have you been doing to that girl?" Myra demanded evenly.

"Now would I do a thing without askin' her?" demanded Barker, and he hiccoughed. "Don't tell old short-shanks. Secret, see. Reached an und-und-understanding. Nice gel that.

Alone. Didn't see the boy-friend. Or did I?" He leaned forward drunkenly. "Don't tell old short-shanks, will yer?"

Topsy reached Myra's side.

"He hasn't been up there long enough to do any harm," she said in a voice which held a touch of venom in it, and was very different from the childish lisp she had used on Wally David-son. "I've been watching him."

"Now, Topshy," protested Barker. " 'Aven't 'ad a li'l drink till now. First today, first yesterday, first since I started coming to this perishing house. Creeps! That's what I got. 'Ad to 'ave a li'l drink, an' made an appoint—appoint—. Goin' out for a li'l drink together tonight. She won't tell ole short-shanks. You won't, either. Good scout, Myra." He stretched out a red paw and would have touched her shoulder, but she moved fastidi-ously away.

"Come downstairs," she said.

"No offence, no offence," said Barker, and he shambled off to the kitchen quarters. Here a narrow staircase led downwards. Slightly sobered, Barker negotiated his descent well enough. Four doors confronted him and when he opened one of them he was met by a thick pall of tobacco smoke.

Seven men were sitting round a table, cards and beer mugs in hand.

None of them appeared surprised to see Barker, nor Myra, who had slipped through behind him.

They eyed her, however, a little warily.

There was nothing remarkable about any of them, unless it was the fact that their sallow complexions and dark, oiled hair looked distinctly un-British.

"'Lo, sister," said the man nearest Myra, and his voice held an unmistakable American accent. "What's the play?"

"You're to be ready for work at any time," she said, "and

don't get drunk in the meanwhile. What do you think he would have said had he come instead of me."

"Aw, can it, we gotta live. He's not around, is he?"

"He might have been," Myra said dispassionately, "and he told you all to lay off drink until after we'd finished."

"We got a spot tired of being kicked around doing damn-all," grumbled the spokesman. "What're you drinking, sister?"

"I'm not," she said. "If you take my advice you'll put that stuff away and get sobered up."

She did not speak again but went out, followed by Topsy. She went into a second room, furnished as a lounge, and sat down heavily in an easy chair. The midget woman moved to a cabinet and poured a stiff whisky and soda. She handed it to Myra. "You're more than an hour late. What kept you?"

"I had an accident—nothing much—and I had to come a long way round," said Myra. "How long have they been drinking?"

"Since they heard of the trouble at the Landon," she said.

"How did they get to know?"

"Barker went out and brought papers back."

"Damn him," said Myra thinly. "He'll see us played out if he goes on like that." She ran her fingers through her hair. "God, I'm tired!"

"You look it," said Topsy sharply. "Get some sleep while you can, I'll keep an eye on the others."

"Too risky—he might be sending for us," said Myra. "He's going to work again tonight or tomorrow. I could do with something to eat," she added, and the midget nodded and slipped out of the room. She had gone for little more than ten minutes when she returned, her face strained and white.

"There are men in the grounds," she said urgently. "In uniform—Home Guards, I think."

Myra stood up quickly.

"How many?"

"Most of a dozen."

"Tell the others," snapped Myra. She ran to the door and up the stairs, and then to the first floor. From the landing windows she could see most of the grounds of Larch House, and what she saw worried her. The Home Guards were approaching the house from all directions, spaced out at intervals of ten or fifteen yards.

Her breath came unevenly.

Two of the olive-skinned men pelted up the stairs carrying machine-guns, of the type which had been used with such devastating effect at the Landon Hotel. They disappeared, moving silently on the bare boards, while Myra saw two others in the hall, and knew that every approach to the house was guarded.

Her breathing grew sharper.

She turned and hurried downstairs again, making for the telephone. It was a privately-built extension installed at a small cottage half-a-mile away.

She banged the receiver up and down.

There was no answer, and the earpiece seemed dead. There was a touch of desperation in her manner as she tried again, but the line was dead, and she knew that it had been cut.

She licked her lips, her beauty wiped out by fear.

Fumbling in a cabinet she withdrew two small automatics. She checked them to see that they were loaded, and then returned to the first floor.

One of the men called out: "They're getting close. We going to let them have it?"

"Yes, and then get away."

"Okay," he said, and his hand tightened on the machinegun.

The landing was the best place in the house for watching,

for she could see three sides of the garden. In sight were at least a dozen men, the nearest no more than thirty yards away. She knew they were being covered, and that the gunmen in the house would choose the right moment for shooting. The rifles in the hands of the Home Guards seemed pitiably insufficient.

"Okay," the man said again.

He picked out three of the Home Guard, and his companion on the other side of the landing picked out three more. As they opened fire the *tap-tap-tap* of guns came from downstairs as well. One Guard staggered and fell forward—but only one. The rest of them seemed well trained in the art of defence.

Some fell flat, others dodged swiftly to trees which gave them cover, and the hail of bullets did little more than peck at the long grass of the grounds. The movement had been so well considered that it told Myra that the attack had been expected.

She was sure now that the wipe-out which had seemed the only way to secure their escape would not be possible. They would have to fight their way out. And that, she knew, was not going to be easy, for from behind the first line of Home Guards, now all completely invisible, there came the shattering bark of Lewis guns. Not one or two, but several.

The first line had been flung out to attract the fire, and the Home Guards were prepared to lay siege.

She knew why.

She knew that the trouble with her car had made it possible for a policeman to recognise her, and that she had been followed, despite her confidence that she had eluded pursuit by a long detour. She had then some idea of the immensity of the forces against which she was working.

The gunmen had moved swiftly away from the windows.

They did not speak, but it was clear that they were facing far more than they had expected.

Myra said quietly:

"One of you had better try to get through, Luke."

"Okay. Which one do you reckon?" He was sneering at her, as if telling her without words that it would be suicide for anyone to leave the house, and that she should know it.

Topsy said simply: "I'll do it. It will be easier for me."

In less than two minutes, and before any further shooting had taken place, the midget appeared by the back door. There was no need for her to open it. There was a small window alongside, and this she squeezed through, hidden by an eave, built to protect the door against rain and wind.

Myra went back to the landing, and waited. The Lewis guns were silent, and there was no sign of movement. Except for the trees the only thing she could see was the outstretched figure of the first Home Guard; he was not moving, and she thought dispassionately that he was dead.

Topsy slipped across a vegetable patch filled with cabbages which had gone to seed. She stood scarcely higher than the tops of them. Farther along the garden were other patches of tall growth, and farther down still there were bushes and shrubs. She glided through them, making no sound, disturbing nothing.

She knew that if she could get through the first line of guards she had an even chance of getting through completely. She went quickly, and suddenly she saw the still, khaki-clad figure of a Home Guard not three yards away from her. He was sprawled forward on his stomach, his rifle held in front of him ready for immediate action. She wriggled forward, very slowly, passing unobserved.

A machine-gun loomed before her, the men manning it

clearly unaware that anyone had left the house. She passed this also, and then began to work her way towards the road.

She struck it fifty yards from the drive entrance, and scrambled through the hedge. That was the most dangerous moment, for if anyone was watching from the road he would know where she had come from. There was a guard, but his back was towards her, and she walked hurriedly and without a sound in the opposite direction.

She knew that in five minutes she would reach a road which led to Guildford on the one side and Farnham on the other; it made no difference to her which way she went provided she reached a town so that she could get word through to the St. John's Wood house.

When at last she reached the main road, she felt it safe to start appealing for a lift. Three cars passed her, unheeding, and then, at last, one slowed down. A large man sat at the wheel, a fair-haired man next to him.

"Hallo, Topsy," said Bill Loftus. Carruthers stretched out a hand and gripped her arm before she could slip away. She did not speak because she could not; she felt frozen into immobility and speechlessness, for there was something in Loftus's eyes which frightened her.

Carruthers kept his grip on the midget but contrived to open the door and pull her through. Another car had slowed down behind them but quickened its pace as the Talbot accelerated. At the wheel of the second car was Mike Errol, and with him were his cousin, Thornton, and the exuberant Martin Best.

"What was that?" asked Mike.

"Didn't see," Mark answered.

In the first car, Loftus slowed down at a road junction where a Home Guard was standing. The man saluted and

193

jumped to the side of the Talbot, staring in surprise when he saw a child.

"Appearances are deceptive," said Loftus grimly. "I'm Loftus—which way do I go?"

"Turn right along here, sir, and the first lot of drive gates will be the ones to Larch House. Careful, there's been some shooting."

"*Has* there," said Loftus grimly.

As he turned into the drive of the house, he heard another burst of machine-gun fire. His lips tightened as he drew up beside a group of Home Guards.

The captain, grey-haired, fresh-faced, began to say:

"Mr. Loftus? I . . ."

And then he too saw Topsy.

Loftus smiled.

"She slipped under your noses, Captain, but that's not surprising. How are things going?"

"They're armed with tommy-guns," said the captain gruffly. "I've lost one man, and I don't want to take too many risks—they'll have to give in quickly enough."

"That's just the trouble," said Loftus. "Will it be quickly enough?" He paused and then went on: "I'm leaving this little creature in your care. Better tie her up, she's as slippery as an eel, and has done quite enough damage. I'm going up to the house, and when I've got in there'll be a way for you people."

"But . . ."

"No buts," said Loftus. "It's vitally urgent, and we've taken chances like this before. I'd like you to have a Lewis gun placed behind us and so that it covers the front door. Fire if I shoot for it. Will you do that?"

The captain hesitated, and then said: "Very good." He thought that the large man was proposing to commit suicide, but he had received strict orders to do exactly what Loftus told him. He made his arrangements—including the tying up of Topsy—while Loftus had a word with the other five Department men. They had their instructions and he knew they would obey them implicitly no matter what the risk.

"Right," he said. "I'm driving up with Carry, then. You follow on foot."

He slipped into the Talbot, and Carruthers slid in after him. The car leapt forward, but it was more than thirty yards from the front door of Larch House when the tommy-guns started, and bullets spattered about them in a hail which it seemed impossible to avoid.

21

SAYS BRADDON

L oftus did not stop driving, although he heard the dull
thud of bullets in the roof and saw three white marks
appear in the bullet-proof glass of the windscreen. Bullets
went through the roof itself and buried themselves in the
upholstery, but the Talbot went on.

He braked a yard or so from the front porch.

The tyres squealed and slithered on the weedy drive. For a
moment it seemed that there was no chance of the bullet-
proof glass withstanding the fusilade directed against it. If he
or Carruthers climbed out they would be mown down at
once.

And then the tommy-gun stopped firing.

Out of the corner of his eye Loftus saw Mike Errol
almost on a level with the front of the car, firing through
the doorway. One of his bullets had knocked the machine-
gunner out, and in the brief respite afforded them, he and
Mark launched themselves at the porch. From the other
side Thornton and Best followed. Behind them the Home
Guard rushed in support, but as Mike Errol reached the

hall he saw that the machine-gun had already been remanned.

Mike fell forward on his stomach.

From behind him his cousin lobbed a hand-grenade, as coolly as if it were a cricket ball, and then he too went flat. Best and Thornton did the same, while from the foot of the stairs there came a blinding flash, as the grenade went off.

The tommy-gun broke into a dozen pieces, and the hastily-piled barricade of chairs and cushions disappeared as if blown aside by a giant puff of wind.

Loftus was the first to reach the landing. He had an automatic in one hand and a hand-grenade in the other. He saw Myra running up the stairs, and yet another olive-skinned man manning a tommy-gun.

Mark Errol shot him from the banisters. Loftus went on, without a glance behind him, the Department men following. As the Home Guard rushed the ground floor there were spasmodic bursts of firing, and the louder crack of rifles.

Down in the cellar rooms Barker had been deliberately shot by one of his own men as he slept.

The dago who had fired the shot turned and emptied his gun at the Home Guards. He wounded one, but the other fired and a bullet went through the gunman's chest.

There was silence but for heavy breathing in the underground chambers of Larch House.

There were footsteps on the first floor and the ground floor, and louder ones at the top of the house. Loftus and Mike Errol were going neck-and-neck along the passages, and twice they glimpsed Myra Berne running before them. They heard her footsteps loud on the bare boards, and their own thundered in her wake.

She reached the door of the rooms where Braddon and Pam were imprisoned. She had a key in her hand, and she found the keyhole with her first lunge. She heard the thundering footsteps behind her, but she did not turn. There was an automatic in her left hand as she threw the door open.

Braddon faced her, Pam just behind him. Both were completely at her mercy. They read death in her eyes, and in the gun which she raised. Braddon uttered a low-pitched cry and jumped forward.

Her two bullets went wide. Before she could level her gun a third time, Loftus reached the doorway.

He fired.

She lost her balance and fell, twisting round as she did so, so that Mike could see her face filled with viciousness and hate.

He was appalled.

To Mike Errol it seemed then as if he were alone in the room with her, just as he had been alone in the lounge at Byng Court. He could remember her loveliness, and the lambent beauty of her eyes. He could remember her low-pitched voice and her red, smiling lips.

Now he saw eyes in which hate and pain mingled and fought for supremacy, and he heard her voice harsh and low-pitched—*so low-pitched that it might have been Skippy's.*

"You . . ." she swore at them, and her left hand with the gun moved a little. "You won't get him, you won't get him, he's beaten the lot of you, he . . ."

And then she turned the gun on herself, and what there had been left of the loveliness of her face went quickly away.

Loftus finished a quick inspection of Larch House, and then joined the Home Guard captain who had set up "field-headquarters" in one of the rooms. On an old saddle-back sofa

Pam was stretched out, quite unconscious. She had fainted when Myra had shot herself.

Braddon was standing by her. His face was pale, but his eyes showed intelligence and a complete lack of fear. Loftus nodded to him, and addressed the captain.

"Those we didn't kill killed themselves," he said. "There isn't one of them alive."

"I was afraid of that."

"They didn't lack guts," Loftus said, and there was tension in his voice. "But we've got to find out a little more before we can get the results we were after." He looked across at Braddon. "Can we hear something about you?" he asked.

Braddon hesitated.

"Who are you?"

"Now, please," said Loftus. "Don't start asking for official definitions—isn't the uniform good enough for you?" He stared coldly at Braddon, but then laughed and dipped his hand into his breast-pocket. "Read that," he said.

Jim Braddon held a note in his hands, one signed by the Prime Minister conferring on Loftus power which could not be rivalled up and down the country. Braddon stared at it, drew a deep breath, and pushed his hand through his hair.

"Well I'm damned," he said. "I haven't the foggiest notion of what it's all about, but . . ." He looked at Pam's white face, cleared his throat and then told his story, simply and without exaggeration.

Loftus was speaking into a telephone from Home Guard Headquarters, Guildford. As he did so, Spats Thornton was writing a record of what had happened, and the Home Guard captain was making out his report. It said simply that they had received a description of the woman who had been seen in Guildford, and her car. The on-duty patrols of the Home Guard had kept a constant watch, and the girl and car had been seen to go to a house believed to be empty. The captain had given instructions for approach after talking to London. A telephone wire had been found leading to the house, and cut. They had been prepared for opposition and protected themselves as much as possible, and their full casualties were two dead and three injured, one of them seriously.

Thornton went into rather more detail.

Loftus said into the telephone:

"No, sir, I don't think there is any chance that word reached the man in London . . . we caught the midget who might have got through. In any case I've telephoned for a cordon to be flung round the house immediately, and no one's to go in or out of the area."

"That sounds all right," said Hershall. "You're coming up yourself?"

"I'd like to be on the spot," said Loftus. "If what I've been told is true, the owner is an eccentric cripple with an interest in art. It doesn't sound as if it could be our man, but the young couple I found here apparently thought that some of his activities were of a dubious nature, and were foolish enough to say so. He sent them here . . . I won't worry you with a full report of that. It's a queer story, and the house should show us something interesting all right."

Hershall said:

"No one else was mentioned?"

"Not yet," said Loftus.

"All right, get it over quickly," said Hershall, and he rang down abruptly.

Loftus turned from the telephone, and took a drink of coffee from a cup which had been left at his side. He nodded his thanks to the Home Guard captain, and promised to look him up in the near future.

The thing which worried him most was the deliberation with which the gunmen and the actress had made sure of death.

The explanation he believed was the simple one; they knew that they were doomed, and they had preferred to kill themselves rather than face the extreme penalty of the law. Myra's suicide had been inspired by similar motives, but . . .

She had *hated* him.

In that there could have been nothing personal; he had not known her. He could assume only that she had hated him for what he stood for, and in the present instant he stood for England. If she hated the country of her birth—he had to prove yet that she was an English national—it could surely be only because she had been tainted with Nazi philosophy. Yet he had come to the conclusion that the Nazis were not in this business.

He shrugged his shoulders as he climbed into the Talbot. The Department men followed him. Carruthers rode next to him, and the others were in the Bentley behind. Three had been slightly hurt, and Carruthers was still bandaged from his wound at the Landon Hotel, although he had suffered little after effects.

He drove fast but with due regard for fellow travellers, his mind working with the cool precision of a fine mechanical tool.

Myra's suicide was the most puzzling factor, but what mattered was to find the connection between an eccentric art lover and the sabotage.

Why had the man changed his secretaries so often?

Was it to make sure that no one knew too much about the records? But it was absurd to think that the man kept a careful record of antiques and record prices as well as the prices at current sales. Yet Braddon said that he did.

The girl said that her guardian rarely bought pieces, and yet he kept his records going at all costs.

The truth was simmering in Loftus's mind, although he had not worked it out in full detail. He was worried in case the man should learn of the disaster, and destroy the records. They covered the whole secret, of course, they must do.

"His" name, Pam had said, was Llewellyn. Owen Llewellyn.

The Talbot was no more than twenty yards ahead of the Bentley when it turned into a road off the Marylebone Road, and was stopped by a policeman. He was one of the cordon flung about the house of Owen Llewellyn.

Loftus was surprised to see Miller among them. The Superintendent was pale, and obviously incapable of exertion, but staunchly insistent on being in at what he hoped was the kill.

"Hallo," smiled Loftus. "A bad omen for the wicked men. How are things?"

"No one's come out of Llewellyn's house," said Miller, "and his two cars are in his garage—the doors are open and they can be seen from the street. I've had inquiries made, and he should have two menservants on the premises, as well as his chauffeur. There are usually three maids, but they went out earlier today—they have their afternoon off regularly on the same day. Nothing unusual in that."

"Nothing unusual for Llewellyn, perhaps," said Loftus, "but it isn't the normal practice to let the staff go off together. However, it's a small point, and suggests that he likes an afternoon and evening when he can do what he likes. He's not been alarmed in any way?"

Miller shook his head.

"Good work. Now Thornton and I are going up to the

house together, and fifteen minutes afterwards your men should close in. The Errols, Carry and Best will start the rush. Whether I show up or not, carry that out, will you?"

"It gives me good time to get all the posts instructed," said Miller. "Anything else?"

"No, just that," said Loftus.

He had no idea what he was going to find, and he knew that there was at least a risk that he would never come out of Llewellyn's house alive. He did not dwell much on that. Spats accompanied him because his knowledge of antiques might prove invaluable; in small things Loftus liked to be sure. Sloppiness in detail could mar a whole project.

They drew up outside the house a minute after Miller's instructions had started to go round, and they lost no time in approaching the front door. Loftus rang the bell. He knew that it was likely that he had been seen from the windows, but he did not think that he and Thornton on their own would cause alarm. There was a long waiting period, and he rang twice again before the door was opened by a medium-sized man whose snow white hair was cut close to his head.

Loftus's eyes narrowed.

He had not seen the man before, but surely there was a family likeness between him and the waiter Farrow of the Landon? The idea pleased Loftus and he stepped blithely into the hall.

"Excuse me, sir, but . . ."

"I want to see Mr. Llewellyn," Loftus said easily.

"He is out, sir."

"Yes?" asked Loftus. "His cars are in the garage."

"I assure you," began the man. But he went no farther, for as Loftus and Thornton stepped towards the stairs they saw a second man standing in the well of the hall. There was an automatic in his hand.

He pointed it deliberately at Loftus, while the white-haired man dipped a hand into Thornton's pocket and removed a gun. It was all done very swiftly and smoothly, and it pleased Loftus, for it suggested to him that the servants were quite sure of themselves and that their employer had not been informed of his arrival. He raised his arms towards the ceiling, but when the man so like Farrow reached him, his right hand moved. He gripped the man's wrist and twisted sharply so that his body came between himself and the gunman. At the same time Thornton knocked the gun from his grasp. It thudded dully against the floor, but there was no report. The gunman opened his lips to shout, but Thornton's right hand gripped his throat and strangled the sound.

Loftus and Thornton moved very quickly then.

With the certainty which came from long practice, handcuffs clicked over wrists and ankles, handkerchiefs were adroitly used as gags, and then silently they started up the thickly-carpeted stairs.

Braddon and Pam had given a thorough picture of the layout of the house, and they mounted the wide stairs with confidence. Half-way up, Thornton said:

"The stuff's all real, Bill."

"So he must be a man of considerable means," Loftus said thoughtfully.

They reached the door of Llewellyn's study. Silently Loftus turned the handle, easing the door open. It was a heavy door, and that suggested it was soundproof. So did the cool, low-pitched voice which came to their ears. There was no hint of alarm in it.

"And so I think it will be wise to make a further demonstration tonight. The message to Hershall will be much more effective if we do that. We must always remember that there still remains the possibility that Loftus will find out the truth, and if that happens of course we can call ourselves finished. Once we get the prices decontrolled, we can sell out to the wholesalers in a matter of twenty-four hours. They will be only too glad to buy."

Loftus and Thornton stood quite still.

Whoever was in the room with Llewellyn grunted, and the speaker went on:

"But for the Department we need not have moved so swiftly, but that man Loftus must be forestalled. I know his reputation, and he, too, is a quick worker. I *think* we have completely deceived him, but we can't be sure. I hope . . ." there was a silky note in the voice then—"you won't hesitate about approving the suggestion. There isn't time to waste."

The other man said:

"I don't want to destroy any more food certainly—we can do with all of it in the country. But, as you say, this is not time for sentiment, so go ahead, Llewellyn. I . . ."

And then Loftus opened the door and went in, showing his automatic, seeing the pale face and the near-black eyes of the man known as Kay, and the fish-like countenance of Mr. Edward Whittaker.

22

FOOD SHORTAGE

Neither man moved after the first turn of the head towards the door. Loftus did not think there was the slightest change of expression on Whittaker's face.

They made no attempt to evade anything. They must have known that what had been said for minutes past had been overheard, and they accepted that fact.

Thornton closed the door.

"Two servants downstairs are quite incapable of action," said Loftus mildly. "And the maids are out, Llewellyn, but you know that. Perhaps I might add a short résumé of what has occurred. Braddon and your ward are in our care. Er—Myra killed herself. There are none of your hired men left at Larch House. This house is surrounded by a force of police at least two hundred strong, and they are closing in." He paused and looked from Llewellyn to Whittaker. "Do I make myself clear?"

Whittaker answered him, his harsh voice giving no suggestion of fear or nervousness.

"So you made it, Loftus. Have I been named?"

"Not yet."

"Is there any proof against Llewellyn?"

"Plenty."

"I see. Loftus, I am a business man, let us approach this crisis in a businesslike way. You're a patriot, I know, and you don't like the idea of endangering food supplies. Well, they're not endangered—I've got enough stored up and down the country to cover all that has been destroyed—I had, and have, no intention of harming the country. My aim was to make a profit. To sell at my own price. By my reckoning I should clear two million pounds and the country will not suffer. Llewellyn was to take five hundred thousand. I am offering you half a million if you'll let Llewellyn and me get away, and hold your tongue for a week."

"I see," said Loftus quietly.

He stared at the man in silence, seeing how everything fitted into place.

"Well?" rasped Whittaker.

"I think perhaps another point of view might make a stronger appeal," Llewellyn suggested. "Whittaker and I have a very considerable supply of food in the country, Loftus, but you don't know where it is, and we do. This is a business proposition, and it has never been anything else. I have given the word for further sabotage tonight—I was prepared to do that without Whittaker's approval. If you don't accept the offer, that food will be gone, and Whittaker's available supplies will not be found. The Government would be wise to spend two million pounds to save one lot and to buy the other. Don't you agree?"

"It's an argument," said Loftus.

The odd thing was that he did not feel it strange that they should talk like that. It was business—dirty business perhaps, but a matter for discussion, and they did not turn a hair as they made and developed their proposition. It might be that they knew the acceptance of it was their one chance of escaping with their lives, but to Loftus it seemed that they had weighed up the risks before, and were disposed to take them.

The ordinariness of it was the surprising thing; they might have been discussing a brokerage deal.

Kay said softly:

"It is a good argument, Loftus. Whittaker has made it clear that there is no intention to harm the country or to injure its prospects. The country will, in fact, be better off—so will we, and if you are wise, so will you. How soon will the police be here?"

"Does that matter?"

"I think so. I shall need five minutes to get away."

Loftus looked at them; he even contrived to smile.

"Gentlemen, there is nothing, now, that either I or you can do about it. The police are closing in, and no one in a widely spread area will be allowed to pass."

For the first time Whittaker showed emotion. The tip of a pale tongue showed against parched and bloodless lips.

Loftus turned to Kay. "To make things doubly sure, Llewellyn, I have discovered that your carefully compiled records of 'antiques', which no one must come to know too well—are the actual records of food stored, and the tabulated warehouses. In code, of course."

Llewellyn drew a sharp breath.

Loftus went on quietly: "Whittaker's stores and whole-depots, working in conjunction with the Ministry of Food, are at least some of the secret dumps, we'll find the others, don't imagine that we won't. Whittaker's men working in the warehouses and dumps which have been destroyed actually did the work of destruction. When did you get these big stores in?"

"I have been accumulating them for many years, I saw this coming ten years ago."

"Very far-sighted," murmured Loftus. "And because of that you thought you had a right to hold a gun at the Government's head. To get your millions you would induce a state of nervousness up and down the country. Men in your stores distributed leaflets, too, didn't they?"

Whittaker made no reply.

"Ah, well," said Loftus, "it was nicely worked out. Llewellyn doubtless thought of the blackmailing of the other directors, that's a little beyond the scope of a plain business man. Yes, very neat—they were all on edge, they could all be guilty. Even Whittaker. But he put himself in the clear by allowing himself to be tortured and knocked out. You were ready to go through quite a lot to get what you wanted, weren't you?"

Whittaker rasped: "I've made you an offer—are you going to take it, yes or no?"

"No."

"Is that final?" asked Llewellyn, and his voice was deceptively gentle.

"Quite final."

"In that case I am afraid we shall all have to go together," said Llewellyn. "I have of course seen the possibility of failure, and I have tried to cover against it. This house is mined, Loftus. I have only to press a button on this desk, and it will be blown up. Even the records." He could afford to sneer; both of them had a coolness of nerve which Loftus would have admired in any other circumstances. "Is that an argument which will make you change your mind, Loftus?"

"Why should it? One life or another doesn't make much difference, and I have already given a full report of what I think has happened, and where the food will probably be found."

"You seem oblivious to the fact that so much more destruction can be contrived tonight," said Llewellyn.

"Somehow I don't think it will be," said Loftus, and he yawned. "Sorry, but I've been busy these past few days."

Llewellyn was moving his hand very, very, slowly. Loftus could not see it move, only that it became infinitesimally nearer to some object on the desk.

Loftus shot him.

He believed the story of the mined house. He believed that Llewellyn could face the decision to bring about his own death and that of all who were in or near the house with equanimity. His bullet struck Llewellyn in the shoulder, and it sent the man back heavily in his chair.

And then Whittaker moved.

He might have reached the door had Thornton not stepped across unhurriedly, and put out a leg which sent Whittaker crashing to the floor. As that happened Loftus moved swiftly, lifting Llewellyn bodily away from the desk to a chair on the far side of the room. None of them saw the door open, not even Loftus.

A voice said coolly:

"Step back, Loftus. And you."

A gun was motioned towards Spats, while the Department men stared at the man in the doorway, at the bluff north-countryman Fortescue. Fortescue's heavy face showed no expression, although his shaggy eyebrows were drawn together in a frown of concentration.

"Keep quite still now," he said. "Ah'm not fooling. Ah've known Whittaker was oop t'something like this for a long time, it's why Ah pretended to work wi' the man Golt. Ah was going to chisel in for a half of the profits, but . . ."

Loftus moved.

He did not know what Fortescue was going to try to do: he

could not understand why the man had shown himself when he might have escaped without direct suspicion. He did not much care. He bent down and lifted Llewellyn again, and the man was as light as a feather pillow in his arms. He just tossed him, as he would a pillow, towards Fortescue. The man was so startled that he lowered his gun, and Thornton moved very swiftly and brought him down from the knees. He and Llewellyn hit the floor together, and Loftus stepped to the desk and sat in front of it.

"The lot, I hope," he said, and he was sitting like that when—three minutes later—Miller and other policemen came in after Thornton had opened the front door. Llewellyn, Whittaker and Fortescue were sitting in chairs and his gun was covering them, while Loftus was looking in particular at Fortescue.

"Spats," he said, "ruffle his eyebrows."

Spats stepped across the room and ran his hand roughly across the north-countryman's forehead. The eyebrows came away with it. Loftus did not know who the man really was, but he did know it was not "Honest Dan" Fortescue; and he was glad.

Treason from Whittaker was quite enough.

Fortescue had been murdered, and his body was found a week afterwards in the grounds of Larch House. His "double" admitted that for some weeks he had masqueraded as the north countryman—his sole purpose being to keep watch on the full activities of the directors. Llewellyn had not trusted Whittaker, and had accordingly taken that precaution.

It was, all in all, said Loftus that same evening, a filthy business. He was speaking to The Rt. Hon. Graham Hershall.

Loftus had made a full report. Not for the first time he was surprised by the thoroughness with which Hershall grasped all details. During the past few days he had seemed to leave everything to the Department, but in fact he had missed nothing.

"There's something else on your mind, Loftus. What is it?"

Loftus smiled slowly.

"Ideas, sir, and . . ."

"All right, let's have 'em."

Loftus said: "It's the mechanical perfection of the show that gets me more than anything else, I think. I've played some peculiar games with the Department, but nothing quite like this one. Right from the start we were *told* where the trouble was likely to be. Arkeld was an obvious suspect—as a source of a leakage if no more. And so while we concentrated on the gentleman, Whittaker and Llewellyn had a free hand elsewhere. Luckily, Craigie thought it wise to check up on them all. If he hadn't we might not have got so far, although the first real lead was from Arkeld, of course."

"Yes?" Hershall leaned forward, took Loftus's glass from a table near him, replenished it with brandy, and then refilled his own. Loftus cupped the glass letting the aroma steal into his nostrils. It gave him a feeling of well-being, and satisfaction.

"We-ell, once we were getting somewhere, Llewellyn put up this gigantic red-herring. Golt, and Germany. He was sure we would fall for it. He arranged with the woman Berne to put up a show with one of our agents, and her apparent death clinched the fact—it seemed—of a Nazi espionage ring. That was all deliberate, to get us off the scent!"

"Hmm. We could have used Llewellyn, I think."

"Ye-es," said Loftus. "We were to be chasing after the espionage angle, while everything was going along nicely for Llewellyn and Whittaker. The idea presumably was that when you saw that money could buy off the trouble, you would pay up."

Hershall put his head on one side.

"And what do you think?"

"I think you would," smiled Loftus. "It was a vast conception that left nothing out, except that there was a mistake which I think is understandable. I was too close to the directors—I managed to get too much too quickly. Fortescue—the false Fortescue—disappeared to try to centre suspicion in that quarter, but apparently I wasn't satisfied, so Whittaker cleared himself—or thought he did. A man who was actually attacked was obviously in the clear—so they thought."

"So did I," said Hershall. "Didn't you?"

Loftus smiled. "There was just one thing wrong about that show, sir. Whittaker was left alive. Arkeld wasn't, remember. They wouldn't want Whittaker to say what had been asked of him, and the reasonable thing was to kill him. They didn't, *and he said they asked him for a plan which they already had.*"

"Well, well, well," said Hershall. "I didn't see that. Each man to his own trade, I suppose. You actually knew it was Whittaker?"

"I thought so."

"You didn't tell anyone."

"I wanted him loose," said Loftus grimly. "There was a chance that we wouldn't find the girl again . . ."

"You thought she was alive?"

Loftus smiled amiably: "That's why I had a call sent out for her, sir. That explosion and the fire was too big a business to kill off one woman, and there was no definite evidence that her body was amongst those of the victims. Yes, a big conception, and a ruthless one. Just one other thing, sir. Who *would* be as ruthless as they were at the hotel? Who *would* be so determined to give nothing away that they would kill themselves? Who *would* in any number distribute those leaflets, and play any part in the sabotage?" He paused, and sipped the brandy. "There was a pretty parcel of hate in all of them."

"Go on," said Hershall.

"Whittaker was a big business man long-sighted enough to get this food tucked away here and there about the country. Llewellyn however thought it necessary to have to stooge at the conference, despite the risk that involved. A vast conception, I repeat. So is world domination, don't you think? I don't believe we'll ever prove it, but if Llewellyn wasn't Berlin's hidden hand in this country I'll eat my hat. The biggest red-herring was to throw the truth at us, believing we would think it too obvious!"

And Hershall said: "That's my opinion too, Loftus. You've done very well. Will we find the stores of food, d'you think?"

"I do, sir," said Bill Loftus; and soon afterwards he took his leave.

It was on the next day that the dumps were found, mostly in Whittaker's stores up and down the country, but sometimes in warehouses and empty houses, a supply greater than that which had been lost. And from the records at the St. John's Wood house there were taken—after heavy work by the cipher department—the names and addresses of the saboteurs; there were eight hundred of them and they were interned for the duration. Against no single one was there any direct evidence, or any clear connection with Berlin. But they would do no more damage.

Loftus was pleased in most ways.

Davidson and Oundle were on the mend, and so was Craigie—who would take a month off when he had recovered enough to travel, and thus have his much-needed holiday. There was a visit from Braddon and Pam to his flat, a couple wrapped up in themselves enough to be touched only lightly by the plot in which they had played so strange a part. Braddon had been fixed up at the Ministry of Food, and they were in their private seventh heaven.

And ten days after the affair at Larch House the B.B.C. announced that the Prime Minister would speak on the Home and Empire Radio that night. He did. Among those who heard him were Loftus and Carruthers, Mike and Mark Errol, Spats Thornton and the exuberant Martin Best, who grumbled at times that he had only had half enough to do in the business.

Hershall refuted the "food scare" leaflet utterly and completely and said there was more food than ever in the country. Yet he treated it as only a brief item in his speech, which concerned the general progress of the war. The six men listening stiffened with the closing words:

"Many work among us, unseen, unknown but unafraid, and to them we owe more than we can reckon. We salute them."

Six men looked at one another; and then six men drank, as if to cover their confusion, to the voice which had just faded from the air.

ABOUT THE AUTHOR

John Creasey, born in 1908, was a paramount English crime and science fiction writer who used myriad pseudonyms for more than six hundred novels. He founded the UK Crime Writers' Association in 1953. In 1962, his book *Gideon's Fire* received the Edgar Award for Best Novel from the Mystery Writers of America. Many of the characters featured in Creasey's titles became popular, including George Gideon of Scotland Yard, who was the basis for a subsequent television series and film. Creasey died in Salisbury, UK, in 1973.

DEPARTMENT Z

FROM OPEN ROAD MEDIA

OPEN ROAD

INTEGRATED MEDIA

INTEGRATED MEDIA

Find a full list of our authors and
titles at www.openroadmedia.com

FOLLOW US
@OpenRoadMedia